# BRUTAL LOVE & STANLEY CUPS

## Book 7 in The Slapshot Series

## HEATHER C. MYERS

## Chapter 1

SHE HAD A BAD DREAM.

It was about him.

Again.

Clara hated that even now, after all of these years, he still managed to haunt her. Maybe it was because Seraphina Hanson had had a job for her and he had been picked up by the Newport Beach Seagulls just before the trade deadline, along with Art Jackman. Maybe it was because now that he was back in Southern California, the chance of running into him on the street was much more possible than when he had been down in Florida.

He probably hated Florida. The guy couldn't stand humidity.

Not that she cared.

Not that she remembered.

Whatever the reason was, the truth of the matter was, she had dreamt of him.

Again.

And she hated it.

The dreams brought back feelings she was sure she had gotten over. It had been years, after all. And their relationship was a whirlwind. It was fast and hard and was over just as quickly as it started.

She shouldn't still be feeling anything for Dean Morgan. It didn't matter that the man was gorgeous in the gruffest of ways. It didn't matter that he had the sort of voice that caused her thighs to get slick whenever he whispered in her ear. It didn't matter that he knew how to touch her in a way no one could ever replicate - which she hated, by the way.

It was over.

At least, that was what she kept telling herself.

Apparently, her subconscious wasn't getting the memo.

Clara cleared her throat and forced herself out of bed. The longer she lingered, the more she thought about the dream. The more she thought about the dream, the more feelings that came from the dream. The more feelings that came…well, it was just harder to stop feeling things completely. And she needed to. Feeling anything for Dean Morgan - even annoyed frustration - wasn't helping the situation. She preferred not to think about him at all. She couldn't allow herself to think about Dean Morgan. The guy was an asshole. Just because they had a history did not mean anything.

She blew out a breath and stretched, hoping to alleviate the tension that had built up so quickly after that dream.

No such luck.

"It's been seven years since I saw him," she muttered to herself, trying to keep her voice as low as possible. "Why the hell…" She didn't finish that thought. She didn't want to wake Bill.

Looking down at her boyfriend of nine months, still sleeping on his side of the bed, she felt her lips curve into a small smile. Bill. She needed to remember that she had Bill now and that was what mattered.

Bill was the guy she wanted to be with.

*Bill.*

Not Dean friggin' Morgan and his asshole tendencies. She

had no idea why she fell for him in the first place, if she was being honest. Sure, the guy was gorgeous. She couldn't deny that. And he had some charm buried underneath his gruff personality.

But she was better than that.

At least, she thought she was.

*You were young*, she thought to herself. *And stupid.*

She clenched her jaw and tried to get comfortable. She crawled back into bed. Now that she had gotten Dean out of her mind, she felt it was safe to do. Her eyes closed and she turned on her side. She tried to relax but her mind buzzed with anticipation. This was almost as bad as her sex dream with Pennywise the Clown from *It*, but at least she didn't have actual experience with Tim Curry so romantic feelings didn't actually linger.

This was not the case with Dean Morgan. She had met him as a high school graduate. It was summer. She thought she could do anything, honestly. There was this sense of freedom that came along with graduation. A sense of accomplishment. A need to go out and start a new chapter of a book that was, as of yet, unwritten. He was ten years older than she was, the epitome of a bad boy in a leather jacket and slicked back black hair. James Dean, but one that swore and undressed her with his eyes, one that whispered dirty promises under the guise of darkness, one that made her feel more special than anyone had ever made her feel before. How could she not fall for that? Even now, she refused to let Bill wear leather. It brought back too many memories.

And honestly, Bill couldn't pull it off the way Dean had.

*No one* could pull that off the way Dean did.

It was almost unfair.

Which was stupid, since that had nearly been ten years ago. It had been one summer with a pro hockey player. A whirlwind romance that had no choice but to fizzle out. Honestly, there was no way they would have lasted. She was young - too young

3

to really know what she was getting into. He was already a veteran player by the time he met her and was focused on his career. They had different priorities. They wanted different things.

It was okay they were wrong.

The problem was, she hadn't gotten over him for the longest time. One of their mutual friends said he took a chainsaw to the sofa the day before he left to go back to Florida for training camp after they broke up.

Thinking about it now, Clara shuddered. They had so many memories on that godawful sofa. If he had really done that...

Maybe he had been affected by the breakup more than she thought.

It was violent, to be sure. And Dean was always a rough guy.

Not with her. *Never* with her. Even when they were fighting. Even when they were yelling at each other and she was pushing his buttons just to make him react. He always said she liked to poke the bar, and maybe that was true. And maybe that wasn't fair.

But he never even raised his hand to scare her.

And that...that meant a lot. It was basic decency, sure, but after her time away from Dean, she realized how little decency existed in the world.

She wondered if the little things she left at his place - a thin scarf she used to wear when she thought she was being so sophisticated, even in the California sunshine; an old pleather jacket she had bought from Forever 21 at Fashion Island to complete the outfit she wore on their first date; her old tooth-brush - made things worse. Maybe he didn't care. Maybe he threw them out like they were trash, yesterday's news. She wondered if he still had them. She missed that scarf and that jacket.

Not that mattered. Those things were material things. She could always get other things. More than that, she had Bill. Beautiful Bill who had nothing in common with Dean Morgan.

Who was polite and nice and they never fought about anything.

Safe.

Bill was safe.

She pulled the cover under her chin, turning away from Bill so she stared at the beige wall currently filled with bleak shadows. Regardless of the reassurances she tried to give herself, she couldn't fall back asleep.

⸻

THE PROBLEM WAS, Bill was an avid Gulls fan. He worked for Grant Winsor as a paralegal who made decent money despite the nature of the job. He was completing his final year in law school at UCLA and would be graduating in the next couple of months before he took the bar exam. Everyone aware of Grant Winsor knew he was an avid Gulls fan - his daughter was even dating first line right winger, Kyle Underwood. In fact, the two were expecting a baby. At least, that was what Clara had uncovered during her investigation. Grant had his own season tickets and his firm also had glass tickets he liked to give out to clients or employees as a way to reward them or to help secure their business.

And tonight was Game 1 in the damn Stanley Cup finals and Bill had glass seats. Clara had managed to avoid attending any game with Bill quite successfully - she had work, she was sick, she was out with her friends. But he purposefully made plans to take her to the game without telling her they were going to it until he turned into the Ice Palace.

Clara had never felt the blood drain from her face before until now. She watched the jumbotron outside light up with the team players. It flashed cutesy little phrases or sayings that encouraged fans to cheer, to get pumped up before coming into the stadium. Lights went out as cars turned off, while headlights sliced through the darkness as drivers searched for parking.

"What are we doing here?" she asked - although yelped was probably a better descriptor.

"I thought I'd surprise you," Bill said, a big smile on his face. "I know you're a Gulls fan, so I didn't understand why you kept avoiding going to the games - even playoff games - with me. But I wouldn't want to take anyone to the finals except you." He grabbed her hand, resting on her lap, and brought it to his lips. "You think we'll get on the kiss cam?"

Oh, God. The kiss cam? She hadn't even thought about the kiss cam. This was too damn much.

*Maybe he won't even see you,* an internal voice pointed out. *Maybe there will be no kiss cam tonight. Maybe Dean will be a healthy scratch. Maybe he totally forgot about you. It's not like he stopped dating after you.*

She snorted. Yeah, right. Dean Morgan might be in his thirties and getting close to retirement age in hockey, maybe he wasn't as fast as he normally was, but the man was still damn solid and gritty as any other twenty-year-old kid. He was good at what he did - more defensive than offensive, but that was why he was paired with Solis. When Solis jumped in an offensive play, he was a reliable defender to watch the blue line.

Until Solis took a cheap hit during the Seattle game and was out for the rest of the playoffs. Now, he was paired with Jackman, which was actually a good pairing since the two were quite similar in style. Art was more controlled, but it helped balance Dean out.

Not that she noticed.

The tickets they had included parking so they found a spot and headed for the rink. It was crowded, which made sense, considering the game was just about to start. Traffic prevented them from making warmups, which made Clara feel like God was smiling down on them. Warmups occurred twenty minutes before the game started. It gave players the opportunity to check out fans, toss a puck over the glass to kids, and just ease into things before the game. Some players, like Petrov, was a laid-back natural at interacting with fans. Dean, on the other hand, barely noticed them. He was too focused. Even girls with tits hanging out of their shirts couldn't catch his attention while he was on the ice. It was like everything shut off in his mind except for hockey.

After walking through security, they headed to their seats. She pulled her motorcycle jacket closer to her. If he had told her they were going to a damn hockey game and sitting against the glass, she would have worn her old UCI hoodie, wouldn't have straightened her hair, or even bothered with makeup. She would have made herself as unnoticeable as possible.

However, considering this was a date, Clara actually put effort into the way she looked. Thank goodness she hadn't opted for that skirt she was going to wear, although she had a feeling Bill probably would have said something.

She wished he had. She would have refused to come. But he knew that - hence why he kept quiet about everything. She wasn't sure if this constituted as something she had a right to be mad about. He was trying to be nice - romantic, even. And he could have taken anyone to this game - but he wanted to take her. That said something.

Bill led her down to their seats. She shouldn't have been surprised when they were at the glass just behind the Gulls' bench, which meant there were plenty of opportunities for Dean to see her. She swallowed as she sat, glad that they had arrived too late to watch warm-ups.

Not that Dean would have noticed, but still.

"Do you want something to munch on?" Bill asked. "I'm going to grab a hot dog."

Was he seriously asking her about food now? After taking her here, to a place he specifically knew she didn't want to be? She tried to keep her glare in check, reminding herself that he was just trying to be polite. He wanted to ensure his girlfriend was fed and satisfied. She understood.

"I'm fine." She hoped her voice didn't actually sound as

shrill as she thought it did. She hoped her voice wasn't as sharp or as maniacal as it came out. "Thank you."

He gave her an odd look but luckily he didn't say anything about it, even when she pressed her teeth together and shot him a smile. It was probably the most ridiculous smile he had ever seen. But he left, nodding his head, probably to himself, leaving Clara alone to breathe.

She started coming up with different ways for how she was going to get out of this. She could pretend to be sick - but stomach issues might not be worth it to Bill for him to leave the game.

*He would*, she thought to herself. *You know if you really wanted to, you could ask him to leave and he would leave. That was how much he loved you.*

Clara took the bill of her hat and pulled it down, hoping it would hide her face even more than it already was. Her temporarily straight hair masked her profile. It had been seven years since she saw him. She was twenty-six now, which would make him thirty-six. They hadn't seen each other, nor talked to each other in that time. Well, save for when Clara saw him on television, playing hockey.

Clara stretched out her legs as best as she could, having seats behind the bench. Luckily, the Zambonis were sweeping the ice and ensuring it was smooth enough to play on. The timer above on the cubed big screen said there was roughly ten minutes until puck drop. Clara knew that meant she had eight minutes before the Gulls were on the ice once again.

She thought about telling Bill her history with Dean Morgan. Part of her wanted to, especially considering she wasn't sure why she was keeping it a secret in the first place. But she worried he might not believe her or assume she was only saying that to try and impress him. Bill was sweet but he was rational and there were times he dismissed what Clara said because he didn't think she knew what she was talking about. She refrained from talking to him about hockey only because she was actually very thorough in her understanding of the sport and didn't want to get into a battle when she pointed out something that he thought was accurate as actually being false.

"I hear he's still single," a voice said from behind her. "Jackman got with that petite blonde chick. I don't remember her name, but Morgan is still single. Rumor has it he likes to pick up women outside after a win so let's hope the Gulls win tonight."

"Candace, we should hope the Gulls win because we want them to win the Stanley Cup," a second voice said. "Not because we have a thing for a veteran defenseman."

The first voice, Candace, snorted. "I honestly don't care one way or the other," she remarked. "All I care about is getting into bed with Morgan. I've been on those hockey forums and the women who have hooked up with him say he's a very generous partner."

"And how do you know those things are even true?"

"I don't, but everything has a grain of truth. At least, that's what my mom always says."

"And do you really want to take your mother's advice?"

"Cheap shot," Candace said. "Look, I don't care about hockey, but Dean Morgan is gorgeous and he's one of the few Gulls that are still single. Even that Russian guy, the one who got divorced last year, is seeing someone. At least I'm not focusing on the guys that are with someone, Ariel."

"How very considerate." It sounded as though Ariel didn't bother to hide her sarcasm if she tried. "Look, my dad gave up his seat because of work. I took you so you could get into the game with me, not to get laid. Doesn't it make you wonder why he's still single? Isn't he supposed to be in his thirties?"

"Who cares, when he looks like that?" Candace said. "I'm going I catch his eye. I wore a low cut shirt for a reason."

Clara pressed her lips together. She didn't particularly care that a woman was trying to get Dean's attention because Dean was not her concern anymore. But she did not need anyone trying to get his attention because that would inevitably bring attention to her.

She glanced up at the clock. Three minutes and twenty-three seconds.

The lights dimmed. The mascot dropped from the ceiling, waving the Gulls flag, getting the entire stadium to cheer and scream. And then, the other team - the Florida Gators - touched the ice, causing the majority of the spectators to stand and boo.

When the Gulls touched the ice, Clara held her breath. She immediately saw Morgan, wearing the number thirty plastered on his back. Fitting, he was playing his old team. Thirty, for her birthday. He still wore it.

Bill got back just in time but Clara didn't notice. As Dean headed to the bench, preparing for the national anthem, he looked up and happened to catch eyes with her.

"Oh my God, he's staring at me!" Candace exclaimed.

Clara wished. But he wasn't. She knew Dean saw her, recognized her, even with the hat and the hair. His eyes still on her as the anthem was sung told her as much.

# Chapter 2

DEAN MORGAN WAS ready to win. Fuck, he was always ready to win. That hadn't changed in the years that he had been playing in the NHL. And now that he was finally here, finally at the Finals, he sure as shit wasn't going to let this opportunity slip through his fingers. He had been working his entire career for this moment, and now, he refused to let it slip through his fingers. He wouldn't let that happen. He was focused, he was sharp, he felt good.

And then he saw Clara, and everything fell apart.

*Fuck me.*

She looked beautiful, the way she did years ago when he got to call her his. Years ago when he knew that body like he knew his, when he got to hear her shower in the mornings and how she would make him coffee and put way too much sugar in it, but he would never say anything because she thought she had some secret coffee recipe. Years ago when she would hide under the blankets during a rare California thunderstorm even in the summer like a fucking child, but it sure as shit made him feel like a man, knowing she trusted him to protect her. Her red hair was straight and her face was half-hidden underneath that Gulls hat but he wasn't stupid. He instantly recognized her jaw, those lips, that small nose. He loosed a breath, trying to look away. He needed to refocus. He needed...

Shit.

He didn't know what he needed right now.

He hadn't expected to see her again. He thought about her every single goddamn day that passed, but he never thought he would see her after he left her. Pain flooded through his chest, squeezing his heart like some bitch who needed to feel his heart bleed into her damn palm. He kept going over this constantly, even years later when he should have been over it, when he shouldn't remember her name much less the fact that there were seventeen freckles across the bridge of his nose.

But shit, of course he remembered everything. It was the one thing he regretted in his life - that they ended in the first place. She should have come with him. Maybe he should have stayed. But they were ripped apart by circumstance and it was the angriest, most depressed he had ever felt in his life. He hated even thinking about it. He was pissed at her, at himself for letting her get away. He was pissed at everything.

He needed to focus.

Dean cleared his throat and shook his head, trying to get his head back in the game. He skated back to the bench, ready for the national anthem while Jackman and his line partners, Underwood, Schumacher, and Ryan, stayed out on the ice, getting in position. They would start the game.

As Dawn Rutgar belted out the national anthem, Dean shook off his nerves. And Clara. Once he stepped on the ice for his first shift, he was fine. The anticipation leading up to that first shift, however, caused his legs to tingle, his body to brim with energy, and he needed to do something active in order to shake it off. It didn't matter that he'd been skating for over thirty years. He still got nervous. He liked to think that nervousness helped him play better, so he welcomed it, even if it did frazzle his nerves.

Or maybe those nerves stemmed from somewhere else.

From some*one* else.

Dean continued to stare at Clara from the corner of his eye even though he didn't want to. He didn't want her to have this power over him, but fuck, she did, and denying that would be like denying that the grass was green or that the sky was blue. He couldn't do it. She completely avoided eye contact; Dean wasn't sure if Clara had was avoiding him on purpose or if she hadn't seen him. But Clara wasn't stupid. She knew more about hockey than any woman he had met, and that fact was still true today. She would know he was on the Gulls. She would know he'd be playing too. Now, whether she actually cared was a different story altogether. Things hadn't ended well for them. He wondered if she was still affected by their relationship the way he was.

Probably not.

But if that were the case, why wouldn't she look at him?

"You ready?" Cherney patted Dean on the back, his eyes on the ice. It snapped Dean out of his thoughts - probably a good thing. "I don't know how it's going to be, Morgan, but don't be afraid to get chippy."

Dean nodded but didn't respond. His focus was on the referee, skating out to the middle of the ice, black puck in his hand. He hoped he was still focused; he hoped he was still ready. But all he could think about - at least, at the moment - was Clara Daniels, the one that got away.

▭

HOWEVER, once he got into the game, he set Clara aside, at least for the time being. He would come back to her later, of course, but unless he happened to see her in his peripheral vision or as he skated back to the bench after completing his shift, he was all in. He had to be, or else there was no way he would be able to leave it all on the ice. And if there was one thing his father taught him, it was hard work and effort were the bread and butter of success.

The first period was winding down and neither team had gotten on the board yet. For now, it was a battle between goaltenders, which put even more pressure on the defensemen to keep pucks out, to make sure they weren't accidentally screening Brandon Thorpe, and to check opponents so they would cough up the puck, which meant skating hard and hitting harder. They also needed to make sure when they cleared the puck, they did it where it hit the boards or a player so it wouldn't turn into an icing call, and the Gulls players would be forced to stay on the ice in their zone rather than rotate in players.

Clearing the puck was actually a skill Dean had that he was proud of. Centers took faceoffs; defensemen cleared pucks, and Dean was able to do so in a way where it did not turn into an icing call against the team.

The irony wasn't lost on Dean as he hopped over the boards to skate probably his last shift of the period. Facing Florida in the Stanley Cup finals, the team he had spent the last eight years with. The reason he and Clara had to break up in the first place.

Not that he was trying to be an ungrateful ass. He wasn't. But going back to Florida was the reason he and Clara had to part ways, and now, he was fighting for the Cup against them. The Gators had traded him at the deadline, and Seraphina Hanson, owner and manager of the Gulls, grabbed him because she wanted grit and experience on her blue line. There was a personal thread Dean couldn't help but tug as he battled with his former teammates, many of whom he still called friend. He wanted to win, wanted to make sure everyone knew what a mistake the general manager made in thinking he was useless, that he couldn't help take the team to the finals. That he was too old or not competitive enough. The worst part of the whole thing was that Florida never actually told him why they were getting rid of him in the first place. It was business. He knew that. It was just business. But it still fucking hurt.

There was no such thing as friend, either, at least when they were on the ice. It was something Dean was good at doing too - compartmentalizing. Before and after, respect was given and received. He could probably take the majority of his former teammates to a bar for a drink, but during the game, they stood in the way of the goal: win. Win, no matter what the cost.

Dean felt more comfortable skating than walking. He dashed to his zone and immediately got in position. Negan had the puck and was skating alongside Drew Stefano and Viktor Jonssan. Morgan and Solis skated just behind them, crossing the blue line into Florida's zone just enough to form a long rectangle with their other teammates.

Negan shot the puck. The goaltender, Hiller, blocked it, and directed a fat rebound to the side. Viktor Jonssan went to pick it up. Negan skated toward the crease, which caused him to get check and shoved by Florida's defense and even Hiller himself.

Dean watched everything unfold, as though he was watching the game as a spectator rather than a player. It was beautiful hockey.

Up until Viktor passed it back to him. Now, Dean was part of this again. Dean stopped the puck but made sure to keep its momentum going so the black disk didn't completely stop moving. He took a hard shot at Hiller once again. Another rebound. All of the Gulls' forwards went for it. Dean hung back just in case it squirted out. Just in case the puck got past everyone. He needed to keep it in their zone, especially when the momentum was with the Gulls. There was chaos at the net. Not even Dean could see what was happening.

The buzzer sounded and the lights started to flash. Somehow, the Gulls had scored.

Negan came flying out from the pack, throwing himself into the boards. Dean, along with everyone on the ice, went to give him a congratulations.

It was so loud in the rink, Dean couldn't hear himself think. His heart pounded against his chest, echoing in his ear. This was it. This was exactly what he wanted. They were up. Dean looked at the scoreboard. Forty-seven seconds left of the period. He hadn't even heard the one-minute warning.

Anything could happen in forty-seven seconds.

It was part of the reason he loved hockey so much. A game could be won in two seconds. A game could be lost in the same amount of time. Which meant there was a lot of pressure on the defensemen as well as Brandon Thorpe in order to ensure another goal did not go in before that buzzer sounded and the period was over.

The Gulls had all of the momentum right now. If Florida scored, that momentum would shift, and the Gators would go to the locker room with more confidence than if they didn't score. Dean - and the team - wanted to hang onto that momentum and do whatever it took in order to ensure they were going to the locker room winning the game.

It did not surprise him that those last seconds were played with both desperation and chippiness. Dean had no problem throwing his body around, knocking the red and blue players out of the crease. He had to be extremely careful, however. If the Gulls drew a penalty, the Gators would be on a power play once the game resumed, which meant they would be rested for twenty minutes, ready to play. The momentum would be on their side.

The clock ticked down. Dean was too focused on the game to even risk looking up and seeing the time. He kept playing, kept shoving people out of the way, kept clearing the puck from the zone, until that buzzer sounded and freed him. It felt like forever, like the longest forty seconds of his entire life, but, like everything, they finally came to an end, and the loud buzzer sounded.

Everyone - Gulls and Gators - stopped playing and proceeded to head into their respective locker rooms. The majority of the crowd cheered, applauding the Gulls as they headed back to the locker room.

Now that he wasn't playing, he had been freed from his spell. His head snapped around and he looked over at Clara as he skated off the ice and to his bench. She was standing but she was standing next to someone. A man. A man who turned his body to talk to her. It wasn't anybody in her family. Dean knew her younger brother and she didn't have cousins, at least on her mother's side. Her Dad and his family lived scattered across the eastern United States. Her mother and brother and one uncle lived in Orange County.

Maybe one of her other relatives came out to spend time with her. That was possible.

Until Dean watched with narrowed eyes as this man squeezed Clara's side with his hand playfully. He was glad to see that Clara did not grin or even react. Her eyes - still practically hidden by her hat - were on him. Her body was unnecessarily tense. She did not know how to react to seeing him, and he felt the same way.

All he could think was, *She's mine, she's still mine, and anyone who says otherwise is going to get the shit beat out of them.*

He wanted - needed - to talk to her, but he wasn't quite sure what to say. He didn't have her phone number anymore; he'd had to get rid of it or he would have been tempted to call every day.

"What's wrong with you?" a gravelly voice asked from beside Dean, snapping him out of his thoughts and forcing him to pull his gaze away from Clara. "You're staring."

Art Jackman. Goddamn Art Jackman and his goddamn timing.

Dean reached up to tap spectators and fans who thrust their hands out of the stadium in order to try and garner a high five as they headed into their locker room before responding to Art Jackman.

"Just thinking," Dean said through a huff once they were safely inside and no one could overheat.

"Thinking with your eyes?" The doubt was evident in his voice.

There were times Dean wanted to punch his own teammates. This was one of those times. Just because Dean had confided in Art a couple of weeks ago, that did not mean Dean was still willing to share what was on his mind. Especially if that person was Clara fucking Daniels, a blast from his past.

"Let's just focus on the game, asshole," Dean said as they stepped into the locker room. He was mindful not to cross the Gulls logo in the center of the floor. He didn't consider himself superstitious but he also wasn't willing to risk it on the off-chance that the superstition was true.

"As long as you can," Art said with a smirk.

Dean clenched his teeth together. Art wasn't just an asshole, he was a smartass, and that was worse than just being an asshole.

Once everyone was in the locker room, Cherney gave his usual speech about trying hard, not to let any of these fuckers walk all over them, and just because they were up by one didn't mean shit because the game could change at any moment.

"Do you want to say anything?" he barked when he had finished, turning his attention to Brandon Thorpe.

Dean raised an eyebrow. Everyone knew Brandon Thorpe didn't say much. He was kind of a snot in that way. He didn't socialize, didn't hang out. He kept to himself. If this was a movie set, he'd be the Method actor, needing isolation to help get into character. In Dean's opinion, it was all bullshit, but Brandon had his respect because he was captain and also because he was a damn good goalie.

"You're doing great," Brandon said, surprising everyone in the room. Every now and then, Thorpe would make a speech, but each time he did, it was like the first: short and shocking. Shocking because he spoke in the first place. "Everyone just needs to keep the Gators out of my zone. You guys are turning it over at the blue line. And D - don't be afraid to get tough with them."

Dean saw the other defensemen nod. He couldn't help but agree. They were playing well but they couldn't make little mistakes because eventually the Gators would capitalize on them. The remainder of the break he was silent, visualizing how he was planning to play in the next quarter. But every time he tried, a familiar redhead would pop up in his thoughts and distract him once again.

## Chapter 3

THE GULLS ENDED up winning by one. Thorpe, as usual, was a beast in the net. Nothing could get past him, even if it seemed like it should. The Gulls played one of their best games to date. Even Clara got into it by the middle of the second period. Just because she had history with one of the players didn't mean she was suddenly not a fan. She had always been a fan. Maybe that was why it was easy for her to forget about Dean for the time being and get into the game.

"That's my girl!" Bill exclaimed when Clara stood up during a brawl. "I knew you'd enjoy yourself!"

Clara bit her bottom lip and ignored the comment. Of course she would enjoy herself. She loved hockey. She loved everything about it. She had just been avoiding it because of Dean Morgan.

*You need to tell him,* a voice in her head admonished. *He's not an idiot. He's going to figure it out sooner or later. It would be best if it came from you.*

And it would, she promised herself. Just…not now. She still needed to figure out how it was going to happen, but it would.

When Negan took a bullshit penalty late in the third, Clara thought this was it. This was the end. They would tie it and have to go to overtime. At least, she wanted to expect that. Getting her hopes up was exhausting, and this type of hockey was more than just competitive. These players were fighting for something that mattered to them, that mattered more than anything else in the world to them *at that moment*.

But it wasn't just the Gulls fighting for this. It was the Gators too. Whether she wanted to admit it or not, the Gators had to be good to get here. A team couldn't just luck their way into the Finals. They had to earn it. And the Gators were fighting just as hard as the Gulls.

What Clara did not realize was that the Gulls would be able to kill the penalty with tired bodies on the ice. They were exhausted. Hell, she was exhausted just watching them. Clara glanced across the ice to see Negan shaking his head and spitting in the box. It was clear he didn't think he deserved the call, and Clara knew it took everything in him not to hit the glass of the box with his stick or to bark back at the refs. Every move the team made was being watched and judged by the refs. They couldn't lose their temper over selfish reasons. Not when so much was on the line.

When they replayed the supposed penalty, it was clear that the referees made a mistake and Sampson dove. Negan hadn't even touched him. Clara wondered if that would garner a makeup call for the Gulls but she realized it probably would not only because there was no time for a makeup call. It might happen next game, but she doubted it. The refs looked at each game like a new game, and that was that. If the Gulls managed to kill off the penalty, there were thirty-seven seconds left in the period, which meant anything could happen. This wasn't like football where the clock could be run down. This was practically a cage match on ice, all with the tension of getting control over the rubber disc and putting it in the back of the net.

During that penalty, Florida pulled their goalie, so there were six players opposing a tired Newport penalty kill rather than the usual five while the Gulls only had four men on the ice.

However, if one of the Gulls managed to ice it perfectly, the puck could potentially go in the back of the net, securing them the win.

Unfortunately for the team and for the fans all standing in the stadium, holding their breaths, darting their eyes between the play and the clock counting down, they were not able to hit the empty net. If anything, the Gulls couldn't seem to clear the puck at all. Everyone in the stadium was on their feet, as if standing could help them see better. Bill had grabbed Clara's hand and held onto it tightly. Neither of them spoke. They watched. The stadium was as silent as it could be.

The minute the penalty expired, Negan shot out of the box and managed to pick up the puck that had squirted out of the zone. He was checked into the boards in the Gator zone, coughing up the puck. He had been so close to hit that empty-netter, but at least the puck was out of the zone and it wasted time on top of that.

The Gators had one more scoring chance. They got into formation and skated down the ice. Their passes were crisp, their skating fast. They were all hulking players - the Gators preferred size over speed, which seemed to work for them surprisingly well, especially since there tended to be a focus more on speed nowadays compared to the old school hockey.

However, it wasn't enough to get past Jackman and Morgan.

Clara couldn't help but smile as she watched the two veteran defensemen in action. She was surprised Cherney had separated them at the beginning of the game, but she also understood it had more to do with pairing two big defensemen together and pairing two small but fast ones together. Each line needed balance. Now, though, they were both on the ice, which made sense, since they both used their bodies and managed to get the Gators to turn over the puck. If the Gators wanted to lean on their size, the Gulls had no problem leaning back.

Dean was an expert at clearing so they got it out of their zone without an icing call. Nobody could seem to score on the open net, however, which meant, until the buzzer sounded and the game officially ended, the Gators had the chance to tie it up and force overtime.

It was the longest thirty seconds of Clara's life. She didn't realize she could hold her breath for that long or bite her bottom lip that hard without really worrying about the consequences. She didn't even feel any pain.

Luckily, the Gators weren't able to score in the remaining seconds of the game.

Thank God that didn't happen.

When the game finally ended, the Gulls mascot waved their silver and blue flag and the ice girls lined up, waving their signature playoff towel in the air. The entire stadium roared. It was so loud, Clara could feel her feet vibrate. Strangers were high giving, kids were jumping up and down.

And to be part of that experience…

It was surreal.

Clara was suddenly grateful Bill had brought her here. Even if it meant she had to see Dean again. It didn't matter. She got to watch a beautiful game of hockey. To her, it was worth it.

The announcer enthusiastically let the crowd know of the Gulls' win and then mentioned the three stars of the game.

"And," the deep voice bellowed over the speakers, "the third star of the game, defenseman, number thirty, Dean Morgan!"

Clara nearly choked on her breath and she faltered in her applause. Suddenly, the world around her started to crumble. She remembered explicitly why she didn't want to be here - even if she was grateful that she was. Bill, next to her, started cheering. He wasn't a huge Dean Morgan fan but even he could agree that Morgan brought a much-needed veteran presence to the team. At least, that was what he had told her after the final buzzer sounded. Not that Clara replied with anything other than an enthusiastic nod. More than that, Dean was big and wasn't afraid to drop his gloves if he needed to. Bill respected guys like that.

Dean skated out without his helmet on, stick in hand. His hair was sweaty, sticky, and Clara felt a sudden rush of adrenaline in her pelvis. He waved it around as thanks to the spectators for being present, for supporting him and the team. And Clara knew what was going to happen next. She didn't know how she knew, but she did. His eyes settled on her and skated straight towards her. Of course, he knew she was there. Of course, Bill wanted to stay until the end instead of leaving right after the game. Dean didn't look at the kids all vying for his attention. The girl behind Clara started freaking out, thinking he was coming for her.

If only he were.

When Dean got to the glass, he pointed directly at Clara so everyone knew she was the one who would receive the stick and no one else, and there was no mistaking it. Even the girl behind her faltered and Clara could feel the daggers being tossed at her back.

"Holy shit," Bill murmured from beside her.

Dean tossed the stick over the glass, his eyes still only on her. He waited to make sure Clara was the one who received the stick and no one took it from her. Bill reached his long arm up and caught the stick before bringing it down and giving it to Clara. Clara barely noticed. Her eyes were locked with Dean's. He lingered for a moment too long before he skated off and the next player was announced.

She knew what that stare meant: this wasn't over. Whatever was between them, whatever tension was still there, had not been forgotten.

"He looked at you like he knew you," Bill said, shouting over the applauding crowd. "Do you know Dean Morgan?"

Before Clara could answer, one of the ushers came to them. "Excuse me," he said in a soft voice. It was hard for them to hear him over the noise. "But you've been invited to get a tour of the Gulls' locker room. May I escort you to the elevators?"

"What the hell?" Bill asked, his eyes wide. His smile was

wide and bright, his entire face lighting up. "Is this something you get when you get a stick from a star of the game? I've never been to the locker room before. Holy shit!"

Clara pretended to be as enthused about the locker room tour as he was. The truth of the matter was, no, just because she got a stick did not mean she was guaranteed a locker room tour. She didn't want it. She wanted to go home and get the hell away from Dean Morgan.

This was Dean. Dean was trying to get to her. If she said no, she would be the worst girlfriend in the history of girlfriends. Because Bill had never been a season ticket holder, he had never gotten an official tour of the Gulls' locker room. More than that, this locker room tour would be given specifically to them by the actual players after a Stanley Cup Finals game. He would definitely wonder why she would turn something like that down, even if she did claim to be sick.

Clara forced a smile, grabbed her stick from Bill, and wondered if he would forgive her if she knocked him unconscious with the stick in order to avoid this whole thing.

However, that was not to be. Bill didn't even ask her if she wanted to take the tour, and, instead, turned to look at the usher and give him an enthusiastic nod.

"Absolutely," he said.

Clara frowned but said nothing. At the very least, she had hoped Bill would take the time to ask her about what she wanted without making the assumption that she wanted to walk around a smelly locker room and accidentally bump into players in suits or players in towels. It was literally just a room with all of their equipment. There was a small room with a television, snacks, and couches just before the actual locker room, and a room filled with sticks before the press room. The showers were to the right, adjacent to the locker room.

The only reason why Clara even knew about that was because Dean snuck her in during the summer - after obtaining permission from Ken Brown, the original owner and manager of the club, before he was murdered - to give Clara her own personal tour before they succumbed to their passion and made love against a wall in the locker room.

Even now, the memory was vivid, racing through her head like a movie. The way his hands touched her body, like her body belonged to him. The way her body reacted because he knew where to touch her and how. She felt herself her flush just thinking about it and shook her head, trying to rid herself of the memory. He probably did this on purpose. Inviting her to the locker room was probably a strategy in order to get her to remember it.

She wasn't going to let him get to her, despite the effort.

Instead, Clara kept her head held high as she followed Bill and the usher out of the stadium and to an elevator. The elevator descended and took them into a small, quiet room.

"Hey Clara," the receptionist said with a small wave.

Bill stopped talking, mid-sentence, in order to give Clara a curious look. "She knew your name," he said. "Was she here when you took that job for the Gulls?"

Oh yes, the job. Seraphina had used her services in order to prove that Alec Schumacher did *not* rape a former ice girl the way she claimed he had. She took the job because it didn't involve Dean and she never saw him once, plus Seraphina always paid her more than her going rate. She wrapped up her job in a week and got paid two grand. She proved Schumacher was innocent and managed to avoid Dean altogether - even with Seraphina innocently bringing him up every now and then.

"Yeah," Clara said, clearing her throat and looking away. She did not need to go into details of why the desk attendant knew her. She had been here for years and recognized Clara from that whirlwind summer with Dean. Thank goodness she hadn't mentioned anything in front of Bill. "Must have."

They continued forward and stepped into the family room, so dubbed because family and girlfriends would hang out here as they waited for their players to finish up with the press and get ready to head home.

Standing outside the entrance, Clara recognized some of the players' girlfriends - Harper, Katella Hanson (and Seraphina's older sister), Emma, and Madison. A petite blonde woman stood with the group. She was someone Clara didn't recognize.

"Clara!" Harper said when her eyes found Clara's. "How are you?"

Clara waved. She didn't want to be rude but any way to avoid mentioning her past with Dean would be helpful. She really didn't want to have to explain herself, especially to Bill who still hadn't even thought to question her about why Dean Morgan had given a grown woman his stick.

Harper didn't know much about Clara and her relationship with Dean, but it wasn't like it was a secret. People talked, and Clara knew that Seraphina and Harper went to college together. Harper had always been polite the few times they had seen each other. Clara shifted her eyes to Bill and then back at Harper. Harper paused and then nodded her head like she understood. Clara felt tension leave her body and she nearly sagged in relief.

"You know Harper Crawford?" Bill asked in a whisper. "You know she's dating Zachary Ryan, right?"

Clara shot him a look. Was he kidding? Of course she knew that, and she didn't appreciate that he was talking down to her. She worked for Seraphina Hanson and she even knew that Seraphina was secretly dating Brandon Thorpe. Not that she would tell that to Bill in order to throw it in his face, as though to prove herself and how she actually did possess hockey knowledge.

"Yes," she said, her voice flat. "Yes, I was aware of that."

Her tone seemed to go over his head.

"I cannot believe we're about to step into the locker room," Bill continued. He opened the door and let Clara walk in before he followed suit. Sam, the backup goalie, sat in a leather couch, dressed in a suit, watching highlights from the game. There were a couple of vending machines off to the side and a table filled with snacks behind the couch.

The door that led directly inside the locker room opened and out strode Dean Morgan, in nothing but grey sweatpants, his body dripping with water like he had just stepped out of the shower.

"Clara," his deep, masculine voice said, his eyes locking with hers before settling on Bill. "Who the fuck is this asshole?"

# Chapter 4

DEAN TYPICALLY DIDN'T CALL fans names. He liked to think of himself as a nice guy. A guy who had some charm, and maybe he could rib someone who could take it, he never went out of his way to be a dick.

That much.

Sometimes, he was instigated on purpose because fans had this odd perception that just because they watched the team play, they seemed to have a personal relationship with the players and could treat them a certain way. They all liked to think that they knew better than professional hockey players and the coaches and if the team just listened to the fans, they'd get easy wins every damn time.

Dean wanted to laugh.

That was bullshit, and everyone knew it.

As it was, the guy in front of him didn't do anything to deserve Dean's ire. Based on the way the guy's eyes lit up looking at the locker room, he was a fan. Dean almost felt bad about antagonizing him until he noticed the guy was holding Clara's hand. And not in a friendly was, but in a *she's mine* kind of way. Dean had no idea how he knew the difference, but he did. And he knew this guy looked at Clara the way Dean probably did.

Based on that, Dean's mind flashed back to when he used to hold her hand. When her soft hand fit within his big one. When she walked out because there was no way she was going to do a long distance relationship and he hadn't thought to ask her to come with him to Florida. When he literally took a chainsaw to the sofa the minute the door shut and he knew she wasn't coming back.

Anger burned through his body, and he was forced to clench his teeth and look away. He couldn't stomach the thought that anyone else had any right to touch her the way he used to.

Why hadn't he asked her to come? Why had he been scared to take that step with her when he knew, even then, that she was the only one for him? That she was the only one he wanted to be with? When she was worth giving up the single life?

Clara cleared her throat, her eyes finding Dean's. Finally. She had been avoiding him all damn night and now decided she could finally regard him with her attention. They were still dark and mysterious, filled with passion. She seemed to disapprove of his name-calling, and even he could admit that it was probably juvenile. But the words just came out. And he wasn't going to apologize for it. The guy was an asshole. He was holding Clara's hand. No one was allowed to hold Clara's hand.

*Jesus Christ, you're really playing into this macho bullshit, aren't you?*

Dean ignored the voice in his head. It didn't matter if it was true or not. It didn't mean shit.

However, he needed to fix his mistake because even if the guy was holding Clara's hand, even if that pissed Dean off, the guy was still a fan. And Dean didn't want to turn him off from the Gulls just because the guy was interested in Clara.

"What I meant was," Dean forced himself to say, though the words felt foreign, like he didn't quite understand why he was saying such things, "hi. I'm Dean Morgan." He stuck out his hand to the asshole still holding Clara's hand. Maybe this would force him to drop it. Maybe he would release his hold on her to shake Dean's hand.

Not that Dean wanted to touch the guy, but anything was better than seeing him with her.

Fucker.

"I didn't know you knew Dean Morgan," the guy said in a low voice, directing his gaze to Clara. However, despite the fact that Dean had called him an asshole, he still dropped Clara's hand in order to shake Dean's. His eyes still glimmered with excitement. "Hi. I'm Bill. I didn't know you knew my girlfriend. Did you meet while she did that job for Seraphina Hanson? Regarding Alec Schumacher?"

Dean shifted his eyes so he could look at Clara. He shouldn't have been surprised that she hadn't said anything to anyone about their previous relationship. There was a chance she wouldn't be believed, and Clara had never been the type to show off or tell people her business. One of the many reasons he loved her. Plus, it wasn't like he told every girl he hooked up with about his previous relationship - the only serious relationship he had had in his entire life.

"Yeah," he said slowly.

There was a part of him that wanted to out her, that wanted this *Bill* asshole to know that she had been with Dean first. Maybe he would get so angry with her, he would break up and she would be single again. But then what? There was a good chance she wouldn't want Dean and he didn't know if he could commit to her.

Well, that wasn't true.

He wanted to. He did. He just wasn't sure what that meant, what that consisted of. And he didn't want to rush into anything only to break her heart again. If that happened, Clara would want nothing to do with him. He knew that the same way he knew how to clear a puck or how to check. And he couldn't risk that.

Dean swallowed and turned back to Bill. He could still feel Clara's eyes on him, trying to read him, trying to figure out what he was planning to say. Hell, Dean didn't even know what he was going to say until he said it.

"Yeah," he repeated. "It was my way of saying thank you. Schu and I are close and I appreciated what she did."

Lie.

Schu was a good kid but if Dean had to pick who he was closest to on the team, it would have to be Jackman. Plus, Schu was an idiot to get tangled into the ice girls. There was a reason that line was drawn in the sand, and while Dean flirted and looked, he didn't even let himself consider getting close to them. It was too dangerous. Quite frankly, he wasn't even that interested either.

"It is so nice to meet you," Bill continued, that big, dumb smile on his face. The guy wasn't even that good looking. What did Clara see in him anyway? He turned to look at her and was surprised to find her looking at him openly.

Bill continued to jabber on but Dean wasn't paying attention to him. His eyes were on Clara's and her eyes were on him. Even now, he could read those eyes like he could read a play developing in an opponent's zone. She wasn't sure what to make of this, didn't know what his endgame was. He could respect that. In all honesty, he didn't know what his endgame was either. He had no idea why he gave Clara his stick or invited her down here for a tour of the locker room. She had already seen the locker room. Hell, he had taken her on the bench next to where his locker room was before. Before he left for Florida. Before he broke her heart - and his, in the process. He was winging it. All he knew was that he didn't want to see her leave any time soon.

He just wanted to see her again. He wanted to be near her. He wanted to be around her. Dean didn't know what to expect. He didn't know what was going to happen but he thought maybe seeing her would...

Fuck if he knew.

He just knew he wanted to see her.

*Pussy.*

"Let me show you around." Dean had no idea if this was the appropriate thing to say. He hadn't been paying any attention to what Bill was saying, but he was pretty sure this asshole would be eager as a damn puppy to look around. And that would keep Clara around Dean too, which was a plus. Even if it meant dealing with Bill longer than he would have liked to.

"Sure, yes, that would be fantastic," Bill said. He pulled Clara along with him, his hand going back to hold onto hers.

At least she didn't appear like she wanted to be here, even with Bill. Maybe she didn't want to be here at all and it was only this fucker who got her down here.

Dean wasn't sure. It didn't matter. If that was the case, then he was grateful. That didn't mean he wouldn't have a problem with Bill holding Clara's hand like it belonged to him.

Dean showed them around the locker room. He couldn't go in the main locker room, where the press was, just yet. Instead, he showed them where the shower was, where the stick room was. At this point, the players began trailing through the locker room with towels wrapped around their waists or in sharp suits. Those that were scratched due to injury were in the suits, having watched the game from the press box.

Bill managed to stop every player he could to grab a picture with him. He didn't ask if Clara wanted to be in them but he had no problem asking her to take the pictures.

"Sounds like a real winner," Dean commented during a picture with Kyle Underwood. Dean, himself, was in sweatpants and a white muscle shirt. He had skillfully avoided the media and hopped in the shower quickly. He wanted to be ready for Clara.

"You don't get to judge my boyfriends," Clara snapped in a whisper as Bill started talking to Kyle Underwood. She held up the phone and took pictures, probably to give her some excuse to do something with her hands.

"Sure I do," he said. "At least find someone who wants to take pictures with you, for crissake."

Dean quirked a brow as he watched Clara take Bill's picture. She had a wrinkle of frustration over her nose - the same one she always got whenever he did something to piss her off and that was a lot of the time.

He felt himself smile at the sight. God, he missed this. More than he missed a lot of things. More than he missed Florida. Florida had helped his career, no doubt about it. He enjoyed the team - even if he hated everyone on the ice now, off the ice was a different story - but he loathed the humidity and actually looked forward to summers because he always found his way back home to Orange County.

"How did you meet this guy?" Dean asked in a low voice. "Did you just need someone so you wouldn't be alone, or did you feel sorry for the guy?"

He watched as Clara clenched her teeth. When obvious pain flashed across her eyes, he knew he had pushed it too far. He didn't have a right to judge her for her boyfriends. He knew that. But something inside of him couldn't stop himself when it came to criticizing her.

"Did that make you feel good?" she asked through gritted teeth.

Jackman seemed to know what was going on because he cruised by Bill and started talking to the guy before Bill mossed on back to Clara. Dean would have to buy the bastard a beer one of these days because it bought himself time with Clara, something he needed. Something he didn't realize was important to him.

"Did that make you feel cool?" she continued. "Congratulations, Dean. I didn't think you could get to be any more of an asshole but you just topped yourself."

"Hey." He placed a hand on Clara's wrist but Clara immediately yanked it away from him.

"No," she snapped. "You don't get to touch me. You don't get to apologize and smile and shrug your shoulders like you didn't *really* do anything wrong. Maybe that would work on other girls but it won't work on me, okay? Please, just leave him alone. You don't realize how much he adores you and this whole team."

"Enough where he completely forgets to offer to take your picture," Dean pointed out. "You think I give a shit what he thinks of me or the team?" He scoffed, shaking his head. "You're not a fucking fool, Clara, so stop acting like one."

He could hear doors opening and closing. From the corner of his eye, he saw Zachary Ryan head out, waving goodbye to everyone. Bill looked up from his conversation with Jackman, almost as though debating on whether or not to interrupt it and go to Ryan or to stay there because Jackman had actually engaged him in conversation. Dean almost smirked in amusement at the sight but he bit it back because smiling while Clara was pissed never ended well for him.

"He doesn't know I'm a fan," Clara pointed out. "That's why he hasn't asked me to take pictures with him."

This caused Dean to pause and raise his eyebrow once again. He shifted his body so he was almost in front of Clara without making it obvious that he was in front of her. Bill didn't seem like the possessive type - he didn't even notice Dean talking to Clara because he was so wrapped up in his conversation with Jackman - but he didn't want to get Clara in trouble with Bill later, even if it meant a potential breakup.

"You haven't told him?" Dean asked.

He wasn't sure how he felt about this. Part of him understood. Perhaps Bill wouldn't believe him. Perhaps it wasn't something she wanted to talk about because she was... ashamed? It hurt too much for her to talk about? Part of him was hurt, though. To pretend that he wasn't a significant part of her life? Was it easy for her to pretend?

"Why would I tell him?" she asked. She turned to look at Dean, her brows furrowed. "I don't go out of my away and talk to people about you. Do you tell people about me?" Dean opened his mouth to say something but Clara cut him off. "Exactly, that's what I thought."

Dean shut his mouth, glaring at her. He had barely spent two minutes with her and already she was burrowing herself under his skin and becoming a pain in the ass, as usual.

"Why did you bring me here?" Clara asked. She glanced over at Bill, who was still talking to Jackman.

Jackman, somehow, entertained this asshole. Dean wondered if Chloe was out there waiting and if she was as patient as she seemed. He wasn't sure how much longer Jackman could deal with him, though, so Dean wanted to jump on it as much as he as could.

"What?" Dean asked, looking down at Clara. He tried to avoid her eyes as much as he could. If he looked into them, he would become weak. He would do whatever she asked if she looked into his eyes.

"Why did you bring me here, Dean?" she asked in a low whisper. "What did you think you were going to get out of this? Why am I here in the locker room?"

"Can't I just want to see you?" Dean asked in a low voice. His voice was filled with honesty and it surprised even himself. She had this ability to bend him and break him and make him more vulnerable than he ever wanted to be.

"No." Her brown eyes were firm. Keeping him out. "When you left..." She let her voice trail off, shaking her head. "I don't blame you for what you did, Dean. Hell, I probably would have done the same thing if our positions were reversed. But when you left, you broke my heart. And I picked up the pieces and moved on. I know you go around and hook up with girls. Again, good for you. You don't belong to me. What I'm saying, though, is you have your life. Do whatever you want. But please, leave me alone so I can live mine."

Dean clenched his teeth together to keep from saying something he might later regret. Clara left to go grab Bill, interrupting his conversation with Jackman. He didn't seem happy with the interruption but when Clara huddled close to him, he rigidly nodded and followed her outside.

She hadn't even looked back at him. He took the hurt and the frustration coursing through his body and pushed it down so he wouldn't feel it. He didn't want to feel anything at all.

# Chapter 5

CLARA DIDN'T CARE if Bill was as pissed as his face made him out to be the minute they got into their car, she was over being around Dean and wanted to leave. She was lucky Billy hadn't actually overheard any of their conversation because, if he had, she would have a lot of explaining to do. Explaining she wasn't quite sure how to even begin. It wasn't as though she had lied to him out right, but even she could it admit it wasn't a good look to keep something so significant from him - even if she didn't want to talk about it.

Her fingers shook as she pulled the seatbelt across her frame and she hoped he didn't notice.

Once they were safely tucked into the car, Bill whirled around and shot Clara an angry look.

"What the hell was that?" he demanded to know. His hands gripped the steering wheel so tight, his knuckles grew even whiter than they already were - and that was saying something.

"I...I told you, I wasn't feeling good," she pointed out, trying to find a believable excuse as to why she would want to rush out of there. She should just tell him the truth. Bill was an understanding guy. She trusted him.

And yet, she couldn't do it.

Not yet, at least.

But she knew after tonight, that window was narrowing significantly. She would have to tell him about her past with Dean...but not tonight. Not when he was this angry.

"If you weren't feeling well, why even come to the game at all?" he asked. His voice wasn't exactly raised, but it did have a tone that made it sound louder than it typically was. He clenched his jaw for a moment, almost like he wanted to buy himself some time to think of what he was about to say before he actually said it. She should appreciate that because she was pretty sure he could hurl a number of hurtful things her way if he really wanted to, and she didn't think she was in the emotional headspace to deal with it right now. The last thing she wanted was to fight with Bill, especially over someone as insignificant as Dean Morgan. "Why allow me to use a ticket on you? I could have taken Cam or Steve, one of the guys at work. They wouldn't have wasted an opportunity to go to the locker room and talk to the Gulls."

"You wouldn't have even gotten to go to the locker room," Clara pointed out. She wasn't trying to be a smarts, but she did want him to realize that maybe he should be grateful that they were even in the locker room in the first place. And that that was all because of her. Sure, Dean probably had selfish motives but still. Bill benefitted...mostly. "I got the stick, remember? Me. Not anyone else."

Clara wanted to say *Not you*, but she had a feeling Bill might not take it that well. She didn't want to insult him.

This made Bill pause and he glanced in the rear view mirror to the backseat where Dean Morgan's stick was. Clara was sure he could see the autograph on the blade in black sharpie. It seemed to settle him down, almost like he was reminded that even though they had to leave the locker room early, they still had some piece of it that they could take home. Something tangible that proved this wasn't some sort of dream. He took a deep breath and looked back at Clara. His shoulders settled slightly, but there was something that told Clara they weren't finished with this conversation, even he was calming himself down.

"I just..." Bill ran his fingers through his hair. "Art Jackman came up to *me*. Me, Clara. He wanted to talk to me. I felt... special. That's been my dream, you know. To talk to these guys like they were my friends. Hell, if I could buy them a beer and shoot the shit with them…that's what I want. I've always wanted to experience that. I've never had such an opportunity before. Whenever they do fan events, it's either too expensive or I can't make it because of work. This is the first time I've been able to interact with them and then, you just…we have to leave. Because of you. And it frustrates the hell out of me because you know how much this meant to me."

Clara sighed. She understood how important this was to him. Maybe she could have waited a little bit, made sure he got the time he wanted with the team, especially after a win in the Stanley Cup Finals. Maybe she had been selfish to get him out of there as quickly as she could, afraid that he might overhear something he shouldn't. Afraid Dean would continue to poke until the truth came spilling out of her mouth.

"I'm sorry," she said, curling her hair behind her ear. She looked down at her lap, crossing one ankle behind the other. "I just… I was feeling claustrophobic in there and I didn't know how to handle myself. I was overwhelmed, if I'm being honest."

He was silent for a long moment before placing a hand on her thigh. She stilled underneath his touch, unsure if he was still mad or if he was getting over it little by little. "Thank you for coming tonight," he said. Clara picked up her eyes up and looked at him, surprised. "I had a great time with you. I wish you liked hockey more; we could go more often. I think you would really enjoy it. I mean, it seemed like you did."

Clara began to fiddle with her fingers. This was the moment. This was what she needed to do. Honesty. Tell him about her past. She could do this. And he deserved to know. If he could be understanding about this, about leaving the tour early even though he wanted nothing more than to stay, she should be able to tell him the real reason they left..

She sucked in a breath, dropping her hands to her thighs, careful not to touch his hand. She wasn't sure how he was going to react and she didn't want to prompt anything inside of him because of her touch.

"Bill," she said slowly. She couldn't look at Bill, not yet anyway. She hadn't talked about Dean with anyone in a long time. It felt completely foreign to her, and everything in her body screamed at her to tell her to stop. But she pushed through, she pushed forward. He needed to hear this. She owed him that much. "We need to talk."

"Uh oh." His hands dropped from her knee and turned the keys in the ignition, starting the car. Ultimately, they fell into his lap. He twisted his torso so he faced her, giving her his full attention. "Am I going to like this conversation?"

Clara smiled a small smile, glad he could find humor in this situation. It was one of the reasons why she loved him; he got over things quickly and didn't hold grudges. She hadn't realized how rare that was until she dated guys before him that seemed to do the opposite. Even if he made her feel bad for leaving, at least he wasn't making her feel bad by being petty and making smartass comments.

"Honestly, it's not really a big deal," she said, "but after tonight, I wanted you to hear it from me."

"Okay," he said with a nod. "Sure." He turned to her so he was giving her his full attention. She appreciated that.

Clara took a deep breath. Even with her seatbelt on, she shifted her shoulders so she could look at Bill directly.

"Dean Morgan and I used to date a long time ago when he played for the Gulls," she said quickly. "Before he got traded to Florida." She held her breath.

Clara watched Bill intently, trying to pick up any tell on his face. He seemed to be trying to let it sink in, and then once that happened, he thought about it. Finally, he furrowed his brow.

"Wait, what?" he asked. "You and Dean?" He cleared his throat. "Look, Clara, I know Dean Morgan gave you a stick. You're beautiful. I tell you that all the time. But just because he gave you his stick does not mean you guys dated. When he was with the Gulls, you were, what, seventeen?"

"How old do you think I am, Bill?" Clara asked. She didn't bother to hide her annoyed tone. There was so many things wrong with what he had just said that any appreciation she had for him had vanished. "I was nineteen. He was twenty-nine. It was the summer before he got traded to Florida. Do you... do you actually think I'm making this up?"

Bill opened his mouth to respond before stopping. He tilted his head to the side, pressing his lips together. Clara knew that look. He made it whenever he disagreed with someone on the radio or any commentary during a hockey game, definitely the referees or whenever the Hollywood Stars played. This was his look of disgruntled agitation.

Clara stopped fidgeting with her fingers and rubbed her thighs with her bare hands. She felt herself get frustrated, wanting nothing more than to react and bite his head off.

"You don't believe me," she murmured. It was as if saying it made her realize that this was true. She blinked when he didn't deny it and sat back in her chair. "Okay. Wow." She looked out of the passenger window. It was pitch black, the only light coming from the street lamps that lit up the nearly-empty parking lot. "You don't believe me." She tilted her head to the side. "Why would I lie about that?"

Bill shrugged his shoulders, shifting in his weight. "I don't know, Clara," he said. "To impress me."

"What?" This time, Clara couldn't help the yelp that came out of her mouth.

"Come on, Clara," Bill said. At least he had the good sense to not even look at Clara. "You know how much I like the Gulls.

Maybe you wanted me to be jealous? I don't know how your mind works. I'm not a mind reader. I just don't understand why you would pick Dean Morgan out of the entire team. He's a lot older than you are."

Clara grit her teeth together but even she could not hold back her anger. "Because I'm not lying about Dean Morgan," she all but shouted.

"No need to react that way," Bill said, his tone defensive. "No need to scream. You can be frustrated with what I'm saying but that doesn't give you the right to yell at me. The least you could do is treat me with respect."

Clara's eyes widened. Was he serious right now? He completely manipulated the situation and made it seem like she was overreacting. She had seen him act this way before, but never with her. She should have known better.

"Bill, I'm telling you this because I didn't want you to find out from anybody else," Clara said. She tried to keep her patience in check - not because she cared what he thought of her, not because she cared how she sounded. It was because she didn't want to be that girl, the crazy girl who went off, even if he deserved it. "Why else would he give me his stick after the game?"

"Because he wanted to thank you -"

"Please." She rolled her eyes. Patience went out the window. The crazy was coming out and she did not care about stopping it. "Does that sound like Dean Morgan? Honestly. When there are tons of fans, tons of kids, wanting his stick, why do you think he would give it to me? That job I did for Seraphina had nothing to do with him. He didn't even know I was there."

Bill gave her a long look, one that seemed to insinuate that what she was saying was not true. "Maybe he thought you were pretty, Clara," he guessed. "Like I said, I'm not a mind reader."

"So you think I made this whole thing up," Clara said slowly, "just to impress you. If that was the case, why would I wait to tell you after we got serious? Why wouldn't I tell you this when we first started dating?"

"I'm not going to play this game with you, Clara," Bill said, shifting in his seat. His fingers flexed before they wrapped around the wheel.

"Why are you so afraid of me dating Dean Morgan?" she asked in a whisper. It made no sense why he would react this way. It had to do with the fact that he was scared or intimidated or *something*. The fact that he was silent, that he didn't believe her, was him in denial. What she didn't understand was why he was in denial in the first place.

"I'm not afraid," Bill snapped, his eyes cutting into hers. He took a breath. "Fine. Let's say I believe you, and you dated Dean Morgan. How did you even get together? What made you break up?"

Clara glanced away, out the passenger window. She probably should have thought about this more. They were valid questions to ask, especially if she had volunteered the information in the first place.

"Dean and I got together after my first year of college," she said. "I tried out to be an Ice Princess and got rejected because I couldn't skate and still can't. He happened to be there and saw me fall flat on my butt trying to scrape off the ice. I think he was there to help bring publicity to it. There wasn't tons of interest because the Gulls were still new and they weren't that great of a team. He helped me up, asked me out, and for three months, we were inseparable, except when he was practicing or training."

Bill scoffed and Clara glared. "Why are making faces if you asked the question?" she asked. "If you didn't want to hear the answer, you shouldn't have asked the question."

"Fair enough," Bill said. He had his elbow on the window sill and his head in his palm, like this was taking all of his energy to deal with.

Clara opened her mouth, ready to continue. Then, she stopped herself and shook her head.

"You know what?" she said. "No. No, it's fine. If you don't believe me, there's nothing I can do to change your mind. You either believe me or you don't, and it sounds like you don't. That's fine. Good to know."

"What do you want, Clara?" Bill asked before groaning. "I'm tired. I had an awesome night that you ruined because you said that you didn't feel good and we left the locker room. The locker room tour - something I had always wanted to experience but never got the chance to until now. And you ruined it."

"I didn't want -"

"You're selfish, Clara," Bill said. "This was a big deal to me. Like, I don't think you realize what a big deal this was to me. And you couldn't just deal with whatever you were feeling for me. You couldn't just do that. Even if you had dated, just put up with him, for me. That's why I'm so upset. Because it doesn't seem like you're sick. It seems like you're feeling good enough to fight with me, just not well enough to let me finish my goddamn conversation with Art Jackman."

"Don't talk to me that way," she said, her voice low and strained. "Do not talk to me like that at all."

"Well, it's getting kind of -"

"There's no excuse, Bill," she pointed out. "Feel how you want to feel. Don't believe me. Think I'm selfish. Whatever. But don't talk to me that way." She unbuckled her seat belt and popped open the car.

"Where are you going?" Bill asked. "Clara."

But Clara was already out of the car. "Sorry for ruining your night," she said. "I'll be back. I just need to be alone."

"Clara -"

Clara didn't stop walking and Bill never got out to stop her. Instead, he drove off, leaving Clara stranded at the Ice Palace.

# Chapter 6

DEAN WANTED TO KICK SOMETHING. He knew that inviting her to the locker room was presumptuous. Hell, he could admit that that probably wasn't a good idea. He knew that he wasn't going to like it when she brought her boyfriend. Because, even when he gave her his stick, he knew that fucking Bill was her fucking boyfriend, even if he wanted to be in denial about it. Even if he had to know for sure. And he knew he wouldn't be able to control the shit that came out of his mouth when he talked to her - because he knew he would have to talk to her. He couldn't be in the same room as she was and not talk to her, even though he probably shouldn't.

"Was that her?" Jackman asked after Clara took off with the douchebag.

Dean hadn't looked away from the door. He wasn't actually sure how long he had been standing there, but it must have been enough for Jackman to fucking concern himself about it. There was still a small part of him that hoped she would turn around and come back. He would consider apologizing, even if he didn't think he didn't do anything wrong.

But obviously Clara wouldn't. That girl was too damn stubborn for her own good, especially if she thought she hadn't done anything wrong. And he sure as hell wasn't going to go after her and make a spectacle. He'd already done enough of that as it was.

"Her?" Dean finally asked.

Jackman nodded, as though that was enough for Dean to understand the situation. The guy was a man of few words. Dean happened to appreciate that most of the time, but other times, it annoyed the shit out of him and he'd want Jackman to just fucking say what he meant without expecting Dean to know what the fuck he was talking about.

"She seems like she has her shit together," Jackman commented. There was a genuineness to his tone. "I tried to talk to him for as long as I could, man."

Dean nodded, running his fingers through his still-damp hair. "I know," he said. "Apparently, I pissed her off."

"Not surprising," Jackman muttered before clapping him on the back. "Good game, see you tomorrow."

Dean was one of the last players out of the locker room. He took another shower and tried not to think about Clara, about the way she still smelled like vanilla lavender, the way he still saw stars in her eyes and fire in her hair. The way she still narrowed her eyes at him and got a wrinkle over her nose. He liked knowing he still had the power to piss her off, even if that made him a dick. The majority of what he did made him a dick, so he couldn't be bothered to care. But knowing he still got under her skin just like he used to…that was enough for him. That was something to be pleased about.

God, he missed her.

He hated knowing that she was with someone else, that someone had the ability to make her happy the way only Dean was supposed to. Granted, the dick couldn't even be bothered to take photos with her in them. Maybe Dean was being biased, maybe he could only see how utterly useless the tool was, but he liked to think that this relationship - whatever it was - couldn't last. Clara would come to her senses and realize that

Bill wasn't the right guy for her. She was a smart cookie; she'd see it.

He got dressed in his street clothes, his hair still damp from the shower. He put his Gulls hat on and walked out the door and up the slope into the parking lot, trying to relax. He should be happier. The Gulls won the first game in the Finals. That was a big deal. But he couldn't shake off this concern of having an opportunity to finally make things right with Clara, and then watching it slip away from him because of his incessant pride, of his need to piss her off just to say he could.

There weren't any lingering fans, waiting for a picture or an autograph, something he was grateful for. He loved his fans, but right now, he just wanted to be alone with his thoughts. Maybe crack open a beer when he got home. Maybe.

He wasn't the type to stew. He liked to throw himself into things, even if it was destructive. Even if they were bad ideas. Maybe he could turn on the television and find some stupid show to watch. Maybe he could shoot pool in his game room by himself while he drank some whiskey. He knew what he'd be in the mood for by the time he got home. He just needed to leave here.

He headed to his BMW when he caught sight of a familiar shade of red hair. He paused and did a quick cursory glance around. Nobody else was with her.

*What the fuck?*

"Clara?"

Maybe he was mistaking things. Shit like that happened to him all the time the first month after he and Clara separated. He thought he saw her in Florida all the time.

It was never her, though. Just her ghost.

His booming voice cracked the silence of the parking lot. Even he jumped slightly at the sound, and he wasn't even trying to be loud.

He narrowed his eyes on the figure, needing to know if he was mistaken yet again, if his mind was playing tricks on him just because he had seen her. Just because he was desperate to see her again, even if that meant seeing things that weren't there.

But the woman glanced up and then tilt her head. She responded to the name. Even though he couldn't see her, he was almost positive she was rolling her eyes and he smirked. Some things never changed.

It was her.

It was really her.

But then, where was her fucking boyfriend? Why was she alone?

It wasn't as though Dean thought the Ice Palace of all places was dangerous. Besides stupid petty shit, Newport was relatively safe in terms of violent offenses. And most crimes were caused by the tourists visiting rather by the actual residents. Plus, security here was topnotch. Still, Dean didn't like the fact that she was by herself. It would be different if she was in her car, but she wasn't next to a car either.

So, that left him back to his original question: *What the fuck?*

"What are you doing out here?" he asked. "Where's your friend?"

Dean would rather be caught with his pants down than call that asshole her boyfriend. He slid his hands in his dark jeans and stopped walking. He didn't want to scare her off by approaching her.

She walked towards him but didn't respond. Instead, she shook her head and looked away. Part of him wanted to reach out and curl stray strands of red hair behind her ear. But he refrained from doing so. He waited.

"If you must know," she said after clearing her throat. "Bill and I had a little tiff."

"And he just left you?" Dean asked, all humor gone from his voice. He clenched his jaw together, his fingers coiling into fists. No, he didn't want to kick something. Now, he wanted to punch something. Or someone.

"I got out of the car, to be fair," Clara said, staring down at her feet. She wore black chucks. Dean would have grinned at how different she was, and how completely the same she was. "I told him to leave. I needed space."

"Space?" Dean crossed his arms over his chest and this time, he did crack a grin. "Lover boy must have done something to seriously piss you off. You don't need space unless you're angry."

"Kind of like when I left the locker room?" she quipped.

His eyes narrowed in on her mouth and he realized how badly he wanted to silence her with a kiss.

"What did you fight about?" He sidled up close to her but made sure not to touch her. He didn't want to be disrespectful and presumptuous. "Come on, you can tell me..."

"Said the big bad wolf." Clara glanced up at him and locked eyes with him. Just staring at Clara made his heart palpitate in a weird pattern. "Not that it's any of your business, but -"

"Hold that thought." He grinned when he saw a flicker of annoyance sparkle in her dark eyes. He loved that look, craved it. "Have you eaten? Are you hungry? I remember you had some kind of wooden leg when we were together. You could put away a torta from Cancun Juice like no one's business."

He heard her stomach growl at the word torta and he grinned. "That's what I thought," he said. "Let me feed you and then I'll take you to wherever you want to go. Even if you want me to take you back to that prick."

Clara opened her mouth, probably to defend the asshole, but she surprised Dean by slowly closing her mouth and letting out a tired sigh. It made him want to wrap his arms around her and ask if she was okay. He wasn't the sort to be romantic because he didn't want romance. But Clara had always been different. That wouldn't change. And he could admit that.

"Is he coming back for you?" Dean asked. "I'll wait with you. I might have to restrain myself from saying something for leaving you by yourself."

"I told him to go," she insisted. "He looked at me like an

adult capable of making my own decisions and respected me by doing as I asked."

"That is such bullshit." He looked around the empty parking lot. "Come on. Let's get you fed. You can tell me all about how wrong you are where we're in a confined space."

Clara didn't resist him this time. Instead, she bit back a smile, crossed her arms over her chest, and followed him. He opened the passenger door for her before circling around to the driver's seat. As he got in, he noticed her feet were on the seat, her arms wrapped around her middle, her seat belt buckled.

Still the same.

"Tell me," Dean commanded.

Clara cut him a look that he easily read as 'don't speak to me that way or there will be a problem' and he gave her a casual shrug.

"I told him," she said, looking down in her lap. Her hair fell into her face, shielding her profile from Dean so he couldn't look at her. He made a right out of the Ice Palace parking lot and headed onto Pacific Coast Highway. "About us, I mean."

"I take it he didn't take it well?" Dean guessed.

He took his eyes off the road only for a moment before looking back out into the dark night. There were only a few cars on the narrow highway, which was a rare sight. Usually, during the day and especially after a game, PCH was jammed with traffic. It was one of the reasons why he typically waited an hour after they played before he even thought about leaving.

"He didn't believe me," she said, finally looking up. From his peripheral, he caught sight of her fingers coiling into tight balls of fists. "He didn't believe me. He thought I was trying to impress him. Why I would pick you, out of everyone I could have a fake relationship with..."

Dean rolled his eyes. "Har, har," he drawled.

"Anyway, I got out of the car and I told him I needed space," she finished. She relaxed her fists and placed them flat on her thighs.

Dean remembered how much she used her hands for things that didn't require them - gesturing, fidgeting. Her nervous tic was playing with her fingers or rubbing her thighs. When she was really worried - like for the final exam she had during her summer courses back when they were together - she would chew on her thumb nail. It drove him batshit crazy.

"And he drove away like an idiot," Dean said, rolling his eyes. Part of him was glad that Bill was an idiot. It gave Dean the opportunity to spend time with Clara alone. However, regardless of his personal feelings for Clara, he didn't think she deserved to be treated that way. It was an odd conundrum to find himself in: appreciating Bill's idiocy and wanting to beat the shit out of him for being an idiot.

"Like I said, he respected my decision."

Dean rolled his eyes. Sometimes, Clara could be so goddamn stubborn, he wanted to scream. He flipped on the blinker and made a right off PCH up Dover before making a left on Seventeenth. He was planning to hit Harbor and grab some food for them. It would probably be close to closing so they could take it to go and eat in the car.

"There's a time to respect your decision and a time to put up a fight," Dean said. "That was a time to put up a fight. No way would I leave you in a parking lot at eleven o'clock at night, even if it's Newport Beach. You get in the car and I won't talk to you but you're damn well getting in the car."

"Maybe that's one of the reasons we're not together," Clara muttered, looking out the passenger side window.

Dean opened his mouth, ready to make a comment, but stopped himself. He let out a frustrated growl and turned onto Harbor.

"Can you call them?" he asked. "I want the usual."

Clara dialed the number and placed the order for them. Dean knew the order would probably be ready by the time they got there. He didn't drive fast. Instead, he took his time and didn't mind it, which was a good thing, considering if you hit a red on Harbor, you should expect the next few lights to be more of the same.

The rest of the ride was experienced in silence, which was the opposite of what Dean wanted. However, he was unsure what to say. He wanted to ask how she was doing but he didn't think it would come across as sincere. He wanted to wrap his arms around her. He wanted to hug her. He wanted to bury his face in her hair and smell her.

God, he missed her. And he didn't know what to do about it.

When he pulled into the parking lot, he murmured to Clara to stay in the car, and went and grabbed the food and the frescas. They just barely made it before closing, and the couple sat in Dean's BMW and started eating.

"Don't worry about spilling," he murmured through a bite of carne asada torta. "You'll probably get it all over your white shirt anyway."

Clara laughed despite herself. "Do you remember," she said, "when we were in San Diego and we were both wearing white shirts, and for some reason, we thought it was smart to go to that hole-in-the-wall Mexican place? And my taco spilled out of the tortilla everywhere?"

Dean's eyes sparkled as he remembered. "The look on your face," he said. "And after that beat, you were over it. You just kept eating. You didn't even give a shit."

"I didn't want my food to get cold," Clara said with a shrug.

"I can't believe you asked for a quesadilla," Dean said.

"They had them, didn't they?" she shot back.

He shrugged and took a long sip of his drink. His eyes found Clara, and for a moment, he watched her eat. Her hair kept getting in her face but her hands were filled with grease and sauce so she tried to move the hair back with her shoulder and it didn't work.

Before he could stop himself, he reached out and curled a strand of hair behind her ear. He had been wanting to do it all night, and he wasn't sure if it was a good decision, but fuck it. He did it anyway.

Clara's eyes snapped up but she didn't move from his touch. She didn't even flinch.

Something passed between them. Something like a spark, a flicker, a shock.

Something was still there between them.

"I, uh." Clara cleared her throat. "You should probably take me back."

Dean nodded but it was the last thing he wanted to do.

## Chapter 7

WHEN CLARA REACHED the door to her apartment, she hesitated. This was stupid. She should just walk in. And she knew Dean was waiting for her to go in. As much of a dick as he could be, there were other parts of him that were more gentlemanly than she expected from him. And if she hesitated, he might get out of the car and come over. And if he did that…

If he did that, there was a chance she might not go back home at all.

She sucked a breath and unlocked the door. The place was silent. She turned and waved at Dean before shutting the door and locking it in place. Flipping on the lights, she wanted to make sure Bill wasn't sleeping it off or something else. It wasn't like him not to be home, and she knew he would have arrived much sooner than she did.

But after a general sweep of her place including the shower and their bedroom, she found the entire place empty.

"Huh."

Clara wasn't sure what to make of that. She wasn't sure where he would go. Bill wasn't the type to go to the bar and drink his sorrows away. It was one of the reasons she was attracted to him in the first place. He wasn't a drinker. He was focused, and determined to eventually make partner at his law firm. He played hockey in an adult league at the ice rink in Yorba Linda. He was fit, attractive, intelligent, and ambitious.

And when they had problems, he knew to grab space and come back with a clear head when both of them could have a civil conversation, be able to listen to each other without getting heated and talking over each other. She expected that he would be here, ready to do just that.

But he wasn't.

She didn't know where he was.

Clara shook her head to herself, wrapping her arms around her body. Bill was perfect. Maybe there were times when he talked down to her or didn't realize she was actually quite familiar with legal jargon because she was a private investigator. Not only that, but she was familiar with hockey because one of her friends owned a hockey team and she used to date a player years ago. He still made her laugh. He made her feel safe in a way where she knew exactly what to expect from him.

And she wanted that.

After her relationship with Dean, stability and a mature partner in a healthy relationship was something she craved.

And the second Dean moseyed back into her life, Clara couldn't see straight.

Did she just fuck everything up with Bill?

She didn't know.

"Dammit," she muttered to herself.

Tears blurred her vision, but she managed to blink them away. She wasn't quite sure why she was emotional over Bill. There was no way he would leave her over this, right? He would let her talk, let her explain herself.

But what was there to explain?

She had told him, and this was how he responded. What more could she say at this point? He either accepted her or he couldn't, and she couldn't force him one way or the other.

That was the scary part.

As predictable as she thought Bill was, she had no idea how he was going to react to this.

She pushed herself from the door and forced herself to take a shower. Clara might have regretted what happened with Bill, but she couldn't shake Dean if she tried. And she hated that. Years had passed between them. It shouldn't be this easy to fall apart at the seams for someone she barely thought about anymore. It shouldn't be this easy to resume their relationship as though they hadn't left each other.

Tears came back into her eyes. This time, her chest tightened, making it painful for her to breathe. She didn't understand why she was feeling this way. She shouldn't. But being around Dean seemed to unlock the Pandora's box of her feelings, feelings she pushed deep down inside of her. Feelings she thought she would never have to deal with again.

Apparently, she was wrong. About everything.

The first thing she did when she stepped into the bathroom was brush her teeth three times. She didn't need Bill to come home and smell the jalapeño and onion on her breath. She needed her mouth fresh and clean. She needed to not remember it that Dean teased her about how she ate the same. If she was going to have a mature, civil conversation with Bill, the last thing she needed was to give him any reason to be upset with her. And if Bill knew she went out to eat with Dean, he wouldn't take that well. Though whether that was because he would be jealous she got to eat with the NHL player instead of him, she couldn't be sure.

When she finished that, Clara turned on the shower and stepped inside. The heat from the water was enough for her to realize that any nostalgia she felt with Dean was not appropriate. She was with someone else. She was in love with someone else. She knew this. Logically, she knew all of this.

And yet, she couldn't get Dean out of her head. The way he looked at her with those sky-blue eyes. The curve of his lips as he gave her one of his patented half-smiles. The way he accidentally brushed her skin with his hand. The way he teased her. The way just the sound of his voice started to get her wet. The way he overwhelmed her with his presence in the best of ways, in a way she clamored for, was addicted to, and only remembered now that she was confronted with it again.

And then, she started crying. She had no idea when the tears started to fall, but they did.

*Don't kid yourself, Clara,* she thought to herself. *You never got the resolution you wanted. Things just ended and that was it. It wasn't like you wanted to break up, and it seemed like he didn't want to break up either.*

She shook her head, her hair sticking to her face and the back of her neck because of the shower. The steam surrounded her face. Dean always said she took showers as hot as the flames in hell —

"Why are you even thinking about him, Clara?" she said to herself. "Bill kind of says the same thing. He should be the one that first popped into your head. Not Dean. Never Dean."

Except that wasn't the case. It was always Dean. She hadn't realized it until now but everything reminded her about the Gulls player. She tried to avoid him. She didn't let herself think about him. When she thought she saw him in a crowd, she reminded herself that she didn't care. When Fox Sports West interviewed Dean during the intermissions of the game, she busied herself with other things so she wouldn't be reminded of how ridiculously good-looking he was, the low timbre of his voice that set her soul on fire, what an amazing hockey player he was. She didn't want to remember it at all.

She stayed in there for as long as she could. It was only when the hot water turned lukewarm and goosebumps ran up and down her arms that she decided it was probably best if she got out.

She dried herself off with a fluffy white towel, trying to warm up her body as best as she could. She wiped the steam off the mirror, looking at her reflection in the mirror.

"What are you doing?" she muttered. "Get a grip."

She wrapped her hair up in a second towel before heading to the bedroom. She pulled on pajamas and let her long hair dry naturally, huffing a sigh. Still no Bill.

"Why hasn't he called?" she wondered aloud.

Except, maybe he had. She hadn't checked her phone in the last hour.

Clara walked back to living room where she set her phone on the dining table. She clicked it on and saw she had three texts from Dean - how he still had her phone number after all of these years, Clara had no idea. She wasn't sure how to feel about the situation. It definitely didn't help when she was doing everything in her to forget him.

But there was nothing from Bill. Part of her wanted to text him just to ask if he was all right. This wasn't behavior that she would have associated with Bill. If Bill was anything, he was considerate, at least of that. The other part of her wanted to give him his space. She also didn't think she had done anything wrong. She didn't feel she needed to reach out and call him or even send him a text. In that respect, Dean was right. He had left her in a parking lot at ten thirty at night, by herself, with no way to get home. Why should she reach out and talk to him?

She headed to her bedroom, phone in hand. She wanted to check Dean's text but wasn't sure if that was the best idea. She didn't need to remind herself that there was some part of her, a small, dark part of her that still craved him. Or, at least, craved closure.

Clara crawled in bed and set her phone on the nightstand next to her. She closed her eyes and tried to fall asleep. The house was still, too still. Deafening.

She turned on her side. The phone stared at her, teasing her curiosity.

She pressed her lips together and switched sides. She felt like Dean was watching her, his eyes heavy on her back. She couldn't fall asleep.

"Okay," she muttered. "Just check the messages and that's it. You don't actually have to respond."

That was a good compromise.

Clara reached out and grabbed her phone, ticking in her passcode and bringing up her text messages.

**What are you wearing**?

Clara rolled her eyes and all but slammed it on the counter. So typical Dean. She knew he didn't know what had just happened between her and Bill but that did not mean she was in any kind of mood to be a target for his jokes.

The phone chirped again.

Clara wanted to ignore it. She also felt her heart race at the prospect of letting herself go off on Dean for all of the frustration that had been building up the past six hours.

She grabbed it and slid it to the home screen before bringing up her messages.

**Just kidding. I know you've had a rough night and I was just trying to make you smile. Probably didn't work.**

Clara felt herself smile despite herself. Yes. Typical Dean. He always pulled shit like that, said the dumbest things at the worst time, just to get some kind of reaction from her. She did believe that he was just trying to make her smile, but he had no idea how to do that. Or he did and his execution sucked.

*You're right on that front.* Clara hit send and waited.

To be honest, she was slightly surprised he even texted her. Not that she questioned his feelings when they were together. He loved wildly and deeply; she had never doubted him. But now? He didn't owe her anything. He didn't need to give her some kind of loyalty, because they weren't actually together. That, and he had a reputation. One that didn't bother her. It had been years. Why would she care if he moved on? Clara was just surprised he wasn't with any of the puck bunnies she knew he'd be able to find by simply walking into one of the trendy bar along PCH.

**How are you?**

Clara went to reply but saw he was still typing.

**I miss you.**

Something warm exploded inside of her chest and dripped down to her stomach.

She deleted what she was going to say, now unsure how to respond.

**Did I say too much?**

He deserved a response.

Well, maybe not deserved.

But she wanted to acknowledge what he was doing. He was checking in on her in his own unique way. And even though it wasn't exactly the way she would have preferred, she appreciated the sentiment because he didn't have to do it. More than that, it wasn't in his nature to do something like that.

But how to respond?

She sighed.

Honestly, she didn't want to talk about tonight at all. She didn't want to talk about Bill or pretend she was okay when she wasn't. In all fairness, Clara had no idea what she was, but okay was definitely not it.

She sighed again. There was something she wanted to ask him after they broke up but never had the courage to because it didn't matter. It still didn't, but she was still curious nonetheless.

*Did you really chainsaw through your sofa before you left for Florida?*

She made sure to leave out the part where he chainsawed through it the night they broke up. She didn't want to talk about them. She didn't want him to know she still thought about him - them - when they used to be together.

There was a slight pause, so much so that Clara clicked back on her phone to see if he had texted back and she just hadn't heard. However, she could see the cloud with the dot-dot-dot inside and she knew he was writing something.

She held her breath; she didn't know why, but this meant something to her.

**Yes.**

Clara waited. Surely he was going to write more than just yes. That explained nothing. Besides the fact that it answered her question, it didn't explain anything at all.

*Oh.* Clara paused, unsure how to move forward. *I liked that couch.*

She wasn't sure what else to say.

**Why do you think I did it? There were too many memories. I needed to get rid of it before I thought any more about you. About what happened on that couch.**

Clara closed her eyes and remembered as well. The couch was worn and used. She didn't know where Dean had picked it up from but she did know he hadn't been the first owner. After a thorough cleaning of the couch, he insisted they break it in. The couch wasn't leather - but it was smooth and comfortable to lie down on.

It would always start innocent. They would watch a movie together, maybe a television show, and he would have his arm around her, his fingers grazing the bare skin of her arm. It always gave her goosebumps. Minutes later, he would scoot closer to her so their thighs brushed and she could rest her head on his chest - which she always did. She loved getting lost in that scent of sweat and Irish Spring. He would kiss the top of her head, his lips would linger, his fingers would stop mid-caress and tighten their grip on her, enough to make a point but not so much to hurt her - he would never hurt her.

And then...

She felt a shudder rip through her body and she took a deep breath. Bill could come in at any moment. If he saw her texting someone this late and it wasn't him...

They would probably be in a long discussion right about now.

Not that Bill had any right to question what she did or to go through her phone, even if he knew the passcode.

**And judging by your silence, I take it you're remembering now too.** He sent her a winking emoji, just to piss her off.

She nearly threw the phone across her room but found herself laughing instead.

**Goodnight, kid. Call me if you need anything.**

*Good night, old man.*

There was no response, but Clara wasn't expecting one. She left her phone on her nightstand and felt slumber tug on her. Somehow, she couldn't bring herself to care about Bill and where he was. She was okay now. As okay as she was going to be, thanks to Dean.

And that was when she could finally sleep.

# Chapter 8

DEAN WAS NOT A MORNING PERSON. He never had been, never would be.

Clara, on the other hand, would wake up at the butt crack of dawn just to do some yoga shit. It always woke him up - or maybe it was the temptation of seeing her bending over in downward dog in nothing but one of his shirts and cute boy shorts that hugged her ass perfectly.

When she was gone, he thought he'd revel in the fact that he would get to sleep in.

But he found he missed the early morning wake up call.

As it was, Cherney was a coach who preferred morning skates early. Earlier than early. As such, there were plenty of times when Dean was late to practice and got reamed by the coach in front of everyone.

This morning was one of those mornings.

In Dean's defense, he had been up all night because he could not stop thinking about Clara. After making sure she was okay - as okay as she could be - he thought he could just crawl into bed and it would be fine.

But that didn't happen.

She was stuck in his head like a damn song he couldn't shake.

He had finally seen her, after all of these years. He had finally touched her, if briefly. He heard her voice, watched her smile, seen that wrinkle on her nose. His heart thumped against his chest. He knew his feelings for her - feelings he had tried to bury and forget about - had crawled back to the surface and held him hostage. Now, he wouldn't be able to look at other women the same way. He wouldn't be able to do things the way he had done before. He was consumed by her, dammit, and he fucking hated it.

But if someone asked him if he would want it some other way with some other woman, he would have told them to fuck off.

Still, life wasn't as easy as it had been, and he had only been with her for a moment. One goddamn moment. A few hours, at best.

Fuck him.

His mind was as scrambled as the eggs she used to burn for him until he kicked her out of the kitchen and made himself in charge of the cooking.

Dean laced up his skates, put on his helmet, and headed to the rink. The bitter chill pinched at his exposed skin. He preferred the cold, but Florida and Southern California - the only two teams he had been part of in the league for the duration of his career - hadn't been particularly cold. As such, he was still getting used to the drastic change in temperature - stepping in from a warm, sunny day into frigid temperatures seemed to wreck havoc on his bones. Jackman told him one time that that was his age showing. Dean told Jackman to promptly fuck himself, but the statement lingered. What if he was getting too old for this shit? Or maybe he was starting to doubt himself now that Clara was back in his life.

Fuck.

This was why he didn't do well with distractions - even beautiful redheads with perky tits and an hourglass frame that he missed holding in his hands.

He shook his head, trying to rid himself of all thoughts of Clara. He needed to focus. This wasn't just any practice. This was more than that. This was for the Finals. He couldn't fuck this up.

Once he got on the ice and got his blood pumping, the coldness - like everything else - vanished and his focus was primarily on the ice.

Thank God.

He wasn't sure if he would be able to compartmentalize the way he used to before.

"Morgan!" Cherney barked from the center of the ice. He wore a helmet over his bald head, his chin strap left undone. He wore a navy blue track suit with the anchor logo in white on the top left of the jacket. "Get your late ass over here."

Dean huffed a sigh and all but rolled his eyes. Cherney might be an old, slight man who was bare five foot ten, but the guy had the vision of a hawk and would be able to spot the eye roll a mile away. If Cherney saw the smartass gesture, he might attempt to teach Dean a lesson by benching him for a game even though it was Stanley Cup finals. That, or he'd make Dean do suicides on the ice, and Dean hated those things with a fucking passion. While Dean typically had no problem rolling his eyes to anyone else under any circumstance, he didn't want to risk missing a game based on his pride being wounded in front of his teammates. Or having his legs burn with contempt because of his demand of Dean.

Dean did as he was told and skated over to Cherney. Cherney ripped into him, as expected, and Dean took it, nodding at the appropriate intervals but not really listening to what he was saying. He already knew what Cherney was telling him - *get his head out of his ass, focus on the game, did he know what the fuck was on the line? Or was he just thinking about some fucking floozy bimbo?*

Dean didn't even bother to react to that at all. He had a bit of a reputation. He understood.

But Clara didn't fit in with that whatsoever, so it didn't matter. Cherney could insult him all he wanted. It wouldn't make a difference.

Not that Dean didn't respect Cherney - he did - but he just didn't want to hear it right now. Not when there was so much other shit on his mind. Besides Clara, there was another game tomorrow. Yesterday had been a tough game, but the Gulls needed to keep up the momentum, especially if they were going to go into Florida's barn in the next couple of days.

Florida had passionate fans that didn't take shit from anyone. They were laid-back, just wanted to kick it with a beer. Yes, there were some crazy-ass people who lived here, but no one could question the passion the fans brought with them to each game. Dean still remembered that even now. Even though he'd been gone for months.

He missed it.

Gulls fans were more fair-weathered. If they were sucking, ticket sales declined. Which he understood.

But still.

There wasn't that same passion, and he missed that. He also knew that could be enough to get into the Gulls' head and fuck everything up for them.

When Cherney has finished seven minutes later, he sent Dean over to Jackman so he could jump into the practice.

An hour later, Dean was left skating, doing suicides for another twenty minutes while the rest of the team watched. Fuck, and Dean thought he had managed to escape that particular punishment. But Cherney was a cruel bastard. If Dean was late a second time for practice during this series, the whole team would be forced to participate.

By the time Dean had finished his punishment, Art was dressed in his typical muscle shirt and jeans, his wild chestnut hair dripping with water from his shower. Meanwhile, Dean's legs felt like they were jelly. He couldn't even stand without shaking and he would be forced to sit somewhere.

Jackman grinned his asshole grin as he watched Dean struggle to make his way to the locker room. Dean had to hold onto the walls to keep himself upright the entire time, and even though he couldn't see Jackman, he could feel the asshole still grinning at him. When he finally got to the doorway, Dean shot him a glare that probably did nothing in terms of intimidation when it came to his defense partner. Thankfully, the bastard held the door open for him.

"Let me help you with that," Jackman said, too delighted for his own good.

"Fuck off," Dean grunted.

Once Dean was in, he collapsed onto the bench and hunched over. He would probably be there for a while until his legs felt like normal again.

"How were your suicides?" Jackman asked in his sandpaper voice. The arrogance in his tone was enough for Dean to look up and contemplate socking his friend in the face. Why Jackman was still here, he had no idea. But he had the kind of face that Dean was in the mood to punch.

Then again, maybe he better not. He didn't want to risk damaging his hand, especially not before the finals.

"Godawful," Dean said.

"Yeah, well, you know how Cherney is." Jackman glanced away, letting the door close behind him, tucking them both inside. "He's always been a bastard, but a fair one." Jackman took a seat next to Dean on the bench. "Thinking about that girl?"

"I fuck girls every night," Dean said, picking his head up to look at his friend. "Clara is a woman."

Jackman smirked. "Good," he said. "You need one of those in your life. Keep your ass in line."

Dean's lips quirked up. He straightened his legs, feeling the familiar tug of his muscles. However, his legs couldn't keep steady. They kept shaking but Dean kept the stretch in place.

"Everything work out okay?" Jackman asked. The arrogance was gone from his tone. He looked at Dean with a serious expression on his face. Dean couldn't be sure but it almost looked like concern flashing across his features. "I know she was with somebody."

"Yeah, that somebody left her in the parking lot by herself," Dean snapped, feeling his fingers curl into right balls that shook nearly as much as his legs.

Maybe he was willing to hit someone after all.

"You kidding me?" Jackman asked.

Dean snorted. "Class act, right?" he asked. "Apparently, he was respecting her decision about wanting space and trusting in her capabilities of getting home by herself." He rolled his eyes and released his hold on his fists, flexing his fingers as he did so. "Can you believe that? I drove her home. Well, I took her to dinner first and then drove her home."

Jackman's brows shot up. "Dinner, huh?" he asked. He shook his head and stood up. "You have a pair of balls, I'll give you that, Morgan."

Dean nodded his head once. He placed his hands flat on the bench and pushed himself to a standing position. He couldn't immediately walk but it was better than before.

"That's what I'm known for." Dean grabbed his bag and slung it over his shoulder.

"Need me to walk you to your car?" Jackman asked, grabbing the door handle and holding the heavy door open so Dean could walk out.

"Don't you have a girlfriend, wanting you home?" Dean asked. He glanced over at Jackman, who caught up with him in two strides.

"Chloe's at work," Jackman replied with a shrug. "We've been together for a couple of weeks now but I want her around all the time, man. I fucking hate it."

Dean snorted. He understood the feeling. Before seeing Clara again, he had thought of her briefly at least once a day. It only ramped up once he was here, where they had first met. Where they had first gotten together. Now that he had seen her, come in contact with her, talked to her, she was all he could think about. Granted, it had only been hours since actually seeing Clara but he didn't think it would mean anything - at least, in terms of thinking of her less.

And he hated it. He hated that there was someone who had such power over him. Clara was the only person he knew of who possessed such power. The women after her meant nothing to him. They were simply a means to an end. Clara... if Clara was his, he wouldn't mind her invading his thoughts and forcing him to think of her all the time.

"So," Jackman said, as they left the rink and walked out into the parking lot. "Did you kick his ass? The boyfriend?"

"I would have," Dean said, "but I didn't want to risk breaking my fingers."

"Bullshit," Jackman said, shaking his head. "That didn't stop you."

"You're right."

A feminine squeak caught his attention and Dean looked up. The players all had a special parking lot just for them that the general public wasn't allowed to use. After practice, it wasn't uncommon to find fans hanging around, hoping for an autograph or a picture. Dean had assumed he wouldn't have to deal with them only because he had stayed late to do Cherney suicides. However, he was confronted with the sight of two women - dressed for the upcoming summer - their faces heavily buried underneath cakes of makeup, smiling and waving at him.

"Enjoy," Jackman muttered, shaking his head.

"They aren't with you?" Dean asked.

Jackman barked out a laugh and slapped Dean on the back.

"I know bunnies don't give a shit that I'm with someone," he said. "But I sure as shit do and I'm making it a point to ignore them. You, on the other hand, are not committed to anything except your dick. And you have made it a point to let them know that. Clowns aren't my types anyway."

Dean smirked and shook his head, giving Jackman a wave as his friend went off to his car. Jackman might have been right about the puck bunnies, because they stood right next to his car.

"Ladies," Dean said as he got closer to them.

Both squeaked, turning to look at each other. From this vantage point, he realized that they were younger than they seemed. He wouldn't be surprised if they were twenty, if that. Suddenly, a large knitted ball twisted and turned in the pit of his stomach. It clenched hard and he was gifted with the ability of having his legs much easier to maneuver around.

"Morgan," they cooed.

"How can I help you on this fine April morning?" He tried to push out his usual charm. He didn't feel it like he typically did, however. It felt forced, almost foreign.

"I think the real question you should be asking is how we can help you," the blonde said.

He chuckled to himself, reaching in his bag to grab his keys.

"I actually don't think I need any help today." The words were out of his mouth before he could stop them. In all honesty, he hadn't expected the words to come out of his mouth, even if they were exactly how he felt.

He saw the women - girls - look at each other, confusion evident on their faces.

"Thanks for swinging by, though." He unlocked his car with a click of a button.

"Wait," the brunette said. "Are you sure?" She stepped towards him. "We heard -"

"I know what you might have heard," Dean said curtly, cutting her off. "I understand why you did what you did. But I'm not interested. Not anymore." He opened his car door and slid inside.

The girls still looked confused, muttering things to themselves. The blonde crossed her arms over her chest, almost as if she was trying to cover herself up, ashamed of what she was wearing.

Guilt surged through him and he nearly cursed out loud. Where the hell had the guilt come from? He shouldn't care how these girls felt. It wasn't his responsibility to make them feel better about themselves. They took a chance trying to seduce him, and that chance didn't work out the way they hoped for. He wasn't going to sleep with them so they felt better about themselves.

*True,* a voice that sounded suspiciously like Clara's, *but you also don't have to be a dick about it either.*

Dean groaned and rolled his eyes. He started the car and rolled down his window.

"Ladies." He stick his hand out of the window to wave them over. He could not believe what he was doing. This was completely unlike him and he hoped his reputation didn't take a hit for it.

*It was a shit reputation to begin with. You should be thanking me.*

He rolled his eyes again just as the women came over to his window.

"Please don't take this personally," he explained. "I need to focus on hockey. You're both beautiful, but I bet you would be even more beautiful without the paint on your face and the skin hanging out of your clothing. You're both better than that, and you can find a better guy to try and impress than me."

He backed up the car and left them in the parking lot. He wasn't sure what the hell just happened, but he definitely knew this was all Clara's fault.

# Chapter 9

CLARA DIDN'T KNOW when she finally fell asleep, but once she had, she slept through the entire night and well into the morning. It wasn't like her to sleep in only because she typically woke early naturally. She considered herself a morning person, after all, and got in a lot of work and exercise while the world was quiet.

This morning was much different. It was as though her body demanded rest whether she wanted it or not. After last night, she understood. Hell, she was grateful for the opportunity to indulge in a few hours of extra sleep. Maybe she'd be in a better mood, and when she and Bill talked about what happened last night, they would be able to listen and understand each other's perspective.

By the time she woke up, the sun was shining through the window and was tugging at the lids of her eyes, trying to pry them apart. When she finally opened her eyes, she forgot, for a moment, that she had been waiting for Bill to come in so they could talk. So they could make up. Instead, she remembered Bill not coming home. She remembered texting Dean. And she remembered being okay. Like she wasn't terribly upset that Bill hadn't shown up last night. Like she could talk to Dean and somehow, he made her feel okay. It didn't make the situation okay, but it reminded her that she could survive something she hadn't expected. She could handle it. And whether she wanted to admit it or not, Dean made her feel better even if he was the indirect cause of what was going on in the first place.

Grunting, she reached for her phone on the nightstand in order to check text messages one last time. Part of her had hoped Bill had texted her, at least letting her know that he was safe. Maybe that he was sorry he left her in a parking lot all by herself at night with her having no way to get home. Maybe he wanted to make it up to her. Another, smaller, darker part of her was hoping she would get a text from Dean. She didn't know what she wanted him to say, but just knowing he was thinking of her, that he acknowledged her the morning after that...

*Stupid. You don't want a text from Dean. That would just complicate this even more.*

More than that, she also know there was no reason for Dean to text her. They weren't together. She also happened to be with Bill. So any desire to receive a text message from another guy - let alone her ex - wasn't one of her finest moments. That didn't mean the desire easily disappeared, but at least she could ratio-nalize where it was coming from.

Clara stood and stretched before padding to the bathroom and turning on the shower. She needed a break from all of this and purposefully left her phone on her nightstand, almost as though she was making a statement to herself. She needed distance, though whether it was from Bill or Dean, she couldn't say. Regardless, she didn't want the distraction. She wanted to take care of herself first. She slid off her clothes and stepped under the hot water, letting the steam hit her face and the water wash away her problems.

She felt herself start to get frustrated by the fact that she still hadn't heard from Bill. Clara had been trying not to think about him, not to think about Dean, but this wasn't even about Dean. This was about her boyfriend leaving her alone in a parking lot.

Even if that was what Clara wanted, Bill shouldn't have respected that. There were certain things he shouldn't push, but ditching her because she was rightly pissed at him wasn't one of them. And he should know that. They had been together for under a year but were already living together so in her head, they were serious. Out of respect, at the very least, he could have shot her a simple text that said he'd be staying at his mother's place and he'd be back later the next day. And maybe ask if she was okay, if she made it home or if she needed a ride. Who cared if they got into a fight? His pride shouldn't be that important to him.

Instead, silence.

*Technically, you could have done the same thing.*

She stuck her nose up at that. The truth was, she felt that since she was the one who got left, he should be the one reaching out, not her. Maybe it was petty but she didn't particularly care.

Clara took in a deep breath, trying to keep herself from getting angry. The water kept falling on her like rain, massaging her skin with its steady beat. He would reach out when he was ready. She couldn't force him to be ready if he wasn't, and she knew they would just get into a fight if she pushed too hard too soon.

*Maybe she should. She'd rather fight with him than feel uncared for. At least if they were fighting, that indicated he cared.*

But she knew she wouldn't. She didn't want to give him an excuse to continue to be mad at her, to justify why he was acting the way he was.

After another ten minutes, she stepped out of the shower and dried herself off. She wrapped a towel around her hair and another one around her body. She grabbed her pajamas from the closed toilet seat, padded out of the bathroom and stepped into her bedroom. A quick glance at her bed and she nearly had a heart attack.

"Shit, Bill."

Clara hadn't even heard him come in. She thought for sure he'd at least let her know so she could come out sooner than she had, but apparently, he was too preoccupied with something.

He stood next to her nightstand, her cell phone in his hand. His shoulders were hunched, like he was looking at something serious. Every muscle was strained.

He didn't even look at her as she clutched the clothes she intended to change into to her chest.

"You scared me," she said in a low voice, trying to catch his attention. She tried to see what he was looking at, what he was even doing with her phone in the first place, but she didn't want to be the one to start the fight, even if this warranted one.

"What the hell is this?" He looked down at the phone before glaring at Clara. He raised the phone so Clara could see what he was referring to. "Clara, what the hell is this?"

Clara furrowed her brow. She was suddenly uncomfortable in so little clothing and wished she had pulled on the clothes before stepping out of the restroom. Granted, she didn't expect Bill to hang out in their room, accusing her of something.

"As far as I know, Bill, it's a cell phone," she said. "More specifically, *my* cell phone. Which makes me question why you're looking at it in the first place?"

"Is there a reason there are text messages from Dean Morgan on your phone from last night?" he demanded, taking a step towards her. "Why is he asking what you're wearing?" He narrowed his eyes. "Do you think that's funny? Is that supposed to be some kind of joke between the two of you?"

Clara's cheeks burned with frustration. She started pacing up and down the room, keeping her arms tightly across her chest. She didn't want her towel to accidentally fall off of her.

"Look," she said, and then stopped. Why was she going to defend herself? The real question was, why was he going through her phone in the first place? She whirled around to face him. "Is there a reason you thought it was necessary to go through my phone?"

"You got a call." He cleared his throat and shook his head. His grip on her phone tightened, judging by the way his knuckles turned a white color. "When you were in the shower. I was going to answer -"

"Why would you answer my phone?" Clara asked, cutting him off. "I seriously don't understand why you would do that, especially after what happened last night."

"Don't deflect," Bill said. "Why do you have Dean Morgan's number in your phone? Why was he texting you?"

"Why are you asking me? Clearly you read them. Clearly you already know."

"Don't be cute, Clara." He gave her that face that pinched his cheeks. Like he was talking to an inept child and trying to spell things out slowly so they understood.

"I told you," she said. She stopped pacing, taking a moment to pause and breathe. "I told you about me and Dean. I told you that we were together. You were the one who didn't believe me. You were the one who left me in an empty parking lot at eleven o'clock last night." She took a step towards him. "You want to know why Dean Morgan was texting me? Because he drove me home. Dean Morgan drove me home because he saw me out in the parking lot by myself."

"It's Newport Beach!" Bill exclaimed.

"I don't care," she responded. "You don't know what can happen. Do you honestly think Newport doesn't have its own share of crime? Are you kidding me, Bill? You know better than that."

"Dean Morgan took you home," Bill stated flatly.

Clara started pacing again. "Isn't that what I just said?" she growled. "He saw me and offered me a ride."

"What kind of ride?" Bill retorted. He tossed the phone on the bed.

"What is that supposed to mean?" Clara said, stopping once again to glare over at Bill.

He threw up his hands and shook his head, as though he

wasn't going to elaborate. At least he had the good sense to not push that further.

"I told you," Clara said, taking a step forward, pointing her finger at Bill. "I told you we had been together. You were the one who didn't believe me. You were the one who drove off. You didn't call, you didn't text. I had no idea where you were all night, Bill."

Bill was silent for a long moment. He picked his head up, his eyes cold. "That doesn't explain why he's texting you," he said in a low, dangerous voice. "That doesn't explain why he's taking you home."

"What do you want me to say?" Clara threw her arms out. Her towel shifted a little and she grabbed the top of it to ensure it didn't slide down her chest. "Do you want me to tell you I'm sleeping with Dean Morgan?"

"Are you?" He sounded slightly hesitant, as though he wasn't sure what to believe.

Clara was this close to slapping him across the face for even insinuating something akin to her cheating on him. She felt angry energy course through her bloodstream and she had to clench her fingers into tight fists and dig her nails into her palms to keep from doing just that.

"I don't know, Bill. Even if I told you, would you believe me? Because clearly, someone like me can't possibly be good enough to get into Dean Morgan's pants. Because someone like me can't possibly date the guy. Because I'm nothing - I mean, not compared to the women he could get."

"That isn't what I meant," Bill said through clenched teeth.

Clara shrugged. "How should I have taken it?" she asked.

"You never answered my question," Bill said. He walked hastily past her, making it a point to avoid touching Clara. Clara turned so she didn't feel especially vulnerable in nothing but her towel. "What's going on between you and Dean?"

"Nothing," Clara snapped before he could explain his question further.

"Those texts —"

"He wanted to make sure I got home safely," Clara said. "Someone wanted to check up on me. You... I don't know what you did. I don't know who you were with."

"I wouldn't —"

"Exactly." She leveled a glare at Bill, making sure he understood what she meant. "How does it feel to be accused of something you didn't do? To be accused of something you *wouldn't* do? From someone who loves you and has given you no reason not to trust her?"

Bill raked his fingers through his hair, glancing sideways. "Look," he said. "Can you blame me? Dean is known for breaking up marriages, for sleeping with whomever he wants."

Clara crossed her arms over her chest and shifted her weight from one hip to the next. "So it's Dean's fault?" she asked. "I guess the women aren't responsible for their decisions?"

"Why are you defending him, Clara?" he asked. "The man has no morals, no respect for the rules."

"Rules? What rules?"

"He's just a guy who takes what he wants and doesn't ask," Bill said, shaking his head. He dropped his hands from his jean loops and started to pace once again.

"I thought you liked the guy!"

"As a hockey player, he's an impressive defenseman who can score when he needs to and drops the gloves when the occasion calls for it," Bill said. "As a person, I would rather not call him a friend."

Clara snorted. "You are unbelievable," she said. "You're shredding Dean's character? You? The same guy who doesn't believe his girlfriend when she tells him something serious? Who leaves said girlfriend by herself in a parking lot at night with no way to get home other than a cellphone? I think you're the last person to judge anyone, Bill."

"Why are you defending this person, Clara?" Bill asked,

taking a step forward. "I looked into your relationship. You broke up because of him."

"He was signed by Florida," Clara replied. "What else was going to happen? I was barely nineteen, about to be a sophomore in college. He wouldn't ask me to go with him and leave my life. And I wouldn't ask him to stay and make him give it all up."

"Rumor had it he took a fucking chainsaw to his sofa!" Bill shouted.

Clara didn't understand the anger but she shouted right back. "I don't know, Bill! We only saw each other after all of this yesterday when you accepted his invitation to the locker room. I didn't want to go, but I wasn't going to take what you've been waiting for away from you. I tried to talk to you about it afterward. I tried. But you didn't believe me."

"And somehow, he conveniently swoops in to give you a ride?" Bill asked.

"Yes, he happened to be there," Clara replied. "He was there. You weren't."

"And what did you do?" Bill asked. "What did you do? He just drove you home and then texted you? That sounds like -"

"A friend."

"A friend you used to fuck."

"Years ago," she snapped. "My past is none of your business. All that should matter is here and now."

"What did you do?" Bill raised his voice again, though Clara still didn't understand why he felt the need to yell. She wasn't used to seeing this side of him and wondered if he always had this side, or if it was something new, something she had unwittingly inspired in him. "Last night."

"How many times do I have to tell you?" Clara crossed the room so she could close the blinds she hadn't realized had been left open. "Once again, you don't believe me."

"You just drove?"

"Where were you?" Clara countered, realizing he had never answered the question.

"Don't change the subject," Bill snapped. He started to walk over to her. "What. Did. You. Do?"

"Oh, well he took me to dinner, walked me to my door, and proceeded to fuck me on the bed I share with you. Is that what you wanted to hear?"

Without warning, Bill's hand shot out and slapped Clara across the face. His eyes widened. He hadn't meant do it, she could tell, but he had.

"Clara." His voice softened. He reached for her again.

Clara stepped back. Tears filled her eyes but didn't fall. "Don't touch me," she said, her voice barely a whisper.

She thought about changing but didn't want to risk him snatching her keys or standing in front of the doorway, preventing her from leaving. She would try to make do, change in her car, if she had to. She grabbed her keys and her phone from the nightstand, continued to clutch her pajamas with the other, and stalked towards the door.

"Clara, I —"

Clara yanked the door open, only to come in contact with the crisp blue eyes of Dean Morgan's, his hand in a loose fist, prepared to knock on the door.

# Chapter 10

DEAN LOOKED between Clara and Bill. There was something not quite right going on, but he couldn't put his finger on how he knew that. He chewed his bottom lip and waited. The asshole boyfriend ran his fingers through his hair while Clara had tears in her eyes and her right cheek was splotchy with a red mark. His eyes narrowed and it took him all of three seconds to figure out what happened. The bastard put his hand on her. No wonder he looked ashen. Probably hadn't expected to do it, which meant they were probably in some kind of heated argument. Not that Dean cared. He only cared about Clara, about getting her the fuck out of there so the asshole couldn't touch her again. In any way.

He didn't even hesitate. He took a step forward, his eyes shooting daggers at Bill, who jumped at the step in his direction.

What an asshole.

And a pussy.

Dean curled his knuckles into fists at his sides. He did nothing but continue to glare at the asshole. Part of him wanted to intimidate the guy. The other part of Dean prayed he would put enough pressure on Bill to get him to hit Dean back. He needed that - craved it. Any excuse to punch the guy - one Clara couldn't get mad at him for. Technically, he had a reason. Someone put his hand on Clara and hurt her. Dean was ready to pummel the shit out of him.

Clara put her hand on Dean's chest, taking him out of the moment, causing his thoughts to completely disappear. His eyes unwillingly dropped to Clara and his eyes searched hers. He wanted her permission to hit the guy, but he knew, regardless of what happened to herself, she would never condone that. She was too good for the asshole.

Hell, she was too good for Dean too.

"Take me away," she whispered, her dark eyes pooling into Dean's.

Dean ground his teeth together. His fingers pinched from how tightly they were curled together. His trimmed nails dug into his palms, and he wouldn't be surprised if the angry crescent moons were burned into his palms like tattoos on his skin. Like Clara tattooed his goddamn soul.

He really wanted to beat the shit out of the goddamn weasel, but Clara needed him more and Clara wasn't the type to ask for anything, especially for help.

This fucker was lucky. He should play the damn lottery.

"Fine." His eyes remained firmly on Bill as he got the words out of his mouth. "You come near her again, I'll kill you."

He meant it, too.

Bill seemed to know that because the fucker's already pale face got whiter, like some goddamn Halloween ghost. It would have been fucking hilarious if the circumstances were any different. As it was, Dean was pissed and he doubted he could find anything funny in that moment.

"Dean," she chided but her heart wasn't in it.

Because she didn't mean it, he knew.

Which meant the guy hurt her.

Not just with the slap - it wasn't swollen enough to be a punch - but deep down inside of Clara, she hurt because of him.

It made Dean want to hurt him even more.

He continued to look at Bill, wanting nothing more than for Bill to come at him. Dean wanted to feel threatened in any way he could. It would mean he could defend himself and Dean would go to fucking town on him. Clara couldn't chide him for defending himself, after all. Dean didn't give a shit if he broke his fingers before the big game. He wanted to hear the crunch of his bones, the crack of Bill's knuckles as he popped him back. He wanted to do bodily harm to Bill more than he wanted to do bodily harm to anyone. When he told Bill he would kill him, he wasn't exaggerating and he needed Bill to understand that.

"Let's go," Clara said again. There was a slight urgency in her tone but she had yet to get insistent.

But she was well on her way.

"And you expect me to believe nothing happened last night?" Bill shouted, taking a step towards him. It was like yelling was going to get Clara to stop leaving. Dean wasn't sure if he was trying to have the last word or if he was simply trying to intimidate Clara into staying out, but whatever the reason, Dean was not going to let it happen. "What the hell is he doing here then, Clara? Are you actually leaving with him?"

Dean snorted. Of course the asshole wasn't going to talk to Dean directly. Of course he was solely going to talk to Clara.

Jesus, what a pussy.

What the hell was she doing with this guy in the first place?

"I'm going somewhere where you aren't, Bill." Dean caught the shakiness of her voice, the way she tilted her head down so her hair fell in her face, masking her profile for either of them to see. She was...scared. And Clara didn't scare easily, he knew. "I don't know why Dean is here." She picked up her brown eyes, so dark and filled with flecks of utter sadness that completely gutted Dean as they locked with his gaze. "Please. Let's go."

Dean held her eyes with his and offered her his hand. He nodded once. She was still in just a towel, red hair still wet, obviously from a shower. She took his hand - still so tiny and fragile and soft, just as he remembered it - and he covered hers with his.

"Go change," Dean insisted, nodding at the pajamas in her hand. "I'll wait."

Clara glanced over at Bill, almost as though she wasn't sure if he would let her change.

"Don't worry," Dean said. "He's not going to do anything untoward. I'll be right here, watching his every move, hoping he tries something." He brought his hands up and made a show of cracking his knuckles one by one.

Bill flinched.

Clara disappeared momentarily so she could change. It couldn't have been a few minutes before she was back at his side. She nodded, letting him know she was ready now.

He nodded back.

They began to walk away but Dean heard Bill step out of the door to follow them.

"You can't just leave with him, Clara!" he called.

Clara stopped, as did Dean. Dean whirled back around and in two strides he reached Bill. He glared at him, taking in his lean body shape. Oh yeah, Dean could totally take the guy. He just needed one thing, one excuse, and it would be all over.

"Please tell me again why she has to do any goddamn thing you say." He leaned in close so his mouth was close to Bill's ear. He felt Bill stiffen. Fucking good. The asshole should be scared shitless. "I've always wanted to know - does it make you feel like a man, putting your hands on a woman, a woman you're supposed to love?" Bill pulled his arm back as though he was going punch Dean, causing Dean to grin as he stepped back in order to give Bill more room. "Please hit me. I would absolutely love it if you hit me. I'm begging you. Please."

Bill blanched and took a step back, dropping his hand back to his side.

Dean inwardly rolled his eyes. What a goddamn pussy.

Shame, too. He really wanted the opportunity to beat the shit out of him in a way where Clara didn't get too pissed.

"Clara," Dean said, continuing to stare down at Bill. "Do you need anything before you go? I'm sure Bill will have no problem letting you come back in and get it."

Clara wrapped her arms around her chest and shook her head. From his peripheral, Dean did his best to study her as well as he could while also keeping his eyes fixed on Bill. It was difficult - the only thing he really noticed was the fact that she was visibly upset, trying to curl into herself like a ball. He hated that look on her face. Back when they were together, they had had plenty of fights before - screaming, yelling, and then onto great makeup sex - but she had never been sad because of him before. Disappointed, sure. Hurt, absolutely. But she was never sad, and she definitely never scared.

The fact that she was both right now caused his quick temper to flare once more and he wondered again for the umpteenth time why he couldn't just let himself teach Bill a lesson. He warred inside of himself, trying to figure out what the right thing was in this situation.

*Your anger constantly gets you into trouble*, a small voice pointed out. It sounded suspiciously feminine, with a quality that indicated she knew everything. Clara to a tee. *If you're going to show her that you've changed, now would be a great time to do so.*

"I'm fine," Clara said. Her voice was stronger than he expected, surprising him. In all honesty, he found that he was proud of her resilience. Her damn stubbornness that annoyed the shit out of him when they were together. "I just want to go. Please."

There was that word again. It wasn't as though Clara was rude, but she didn't go out of her way to say it a lot of the time.

Dean stepped back until he was next to Clara once more. Still keeping his eyes on Bill, he reached out and wrapped his arm around Clara's shoulders. He saw Bill glare, saw him open his mouth, ready to argue. Dean snapped his eyebrows up, as though to say, *What? What, exactly, am I doing wrong here? Did you want to say something about my decision to hold her?*

Dean hoped Clara didn't think he was taking advantage of her in her vulnerable state. He hoped she realized that he wanted to protect her, to send a clear message to Bill that his behavior was unacceptable and would not be tolerated. That this was the least of his problems if Dean ever saw him even trying to talk to her again.

By the time Dean led her down to the parking lot where he parked his car in the temporary parking, afraid it might get towed if he parked it in 'reserved' considering this was Irvine and the leasing offices got trigger-happy with towing cars. He opened the door for Clara, not releasing his hold on her until she was getting into his car.

He stepped back, surprised they were here again. For the past eight years, Dean would never have considered he would ever get Clara back in his car again. Now, within the span of twelve hours, he had had her in his passenger seat twice, all because of that asshole boyfriend of hers.

When he got in and he was safely driving - he still wasn't exactly sure where he was going - he turned on the air conditioner. His finger itched to turn on the radio, to fill up this space of silence between them, but he wanted to give her the opportunity to talk if she needed to talk about anything - even if it wasn't about Bill. Even if it wasn't about the red splotchy mark still lingering on her skin.

"You didn't have to threaten his life," she finally said.

"Sure I did," he disagreed, his tone cheery. "Anyone touches you, hurts you, rips one strand of your hair from your delicate head, I will beat the fucker into a bloody pulp. You are a goddamn temple, Clara." He glanced over at Clara even as he drove, locking eyes with her to show just how serious he was about the statement. "A strong woman who deserves to be fucking worshipped. I will not allow anyone to touch you, or talk to you a certain way. And, quite frankly, neither should you."

"What makes you think I would let him talk to me that way?" she asked. She turned her head and he could feel her eyes on his profile.

"I know you wouldn't," Dean said. "You're also very important to me, Clara. I don't know what we are, exactly. What this" - he gestured at the space between the two of them - "is between us. But I know I care about you more than I care about a lot of people."

Clara sighed. He came to a red light and watched her pinch the bridge of her nose.

"What is this, Dean?" she asked. She started twisting her seat belt with her hands. "Whatever this thing is, it's... I don't know. I've been avoiding you since you came here a few months ago. I wanted nothing to do with you, to be honest. I didn't want to feel anything for you. But Bill left me..." She shook her head. "I don't care. I don't want to talk about it. Never mind."

"Still can't make up your mind about anything, can you?" Dean shot her an amused grin, pressing gently on the brake before he made a right turn. His driving was completely on autopilot. He had no idea where he was going but he didn't care. He just wanted to be around Clara.

There was a moment of silence that passed between them. Dean couldn't tell if it was awkward or if it was comfortable.

"Do you want to talk about what happened?" he asked, his voice gentle.

"Not really." She dropped the seatbelt and placed her hands on the leather seat, her fingers curling around the sides.

He nodded once and looked back out his window. He had hoped she would say yes. He wanted her to say yes more than anything. But he had a feeling she would say no only because Clara was the sort who would keep things close to her chest. Even when they were together, she didn't talk much about what was troubling her, if anything. He wanted to make it better but he didn't know how if she wouldn't communicate.

"Hey." He dropped one hand from the steering wheel to cover hers. He could feel all the tension dissipate, at least from her hand, before it became limp in his own. "I know things between us..." He stopped, glanced back at the car in front of him. He had never been that good at saying the right words at the right time. In all honesty, he was better with gestures than with words. "It doesn't matter. What matters is that you and I are..." Another sigh. Another hesitation. "I'm here for you, Clara. You are important to me and I just want you to know that if you need anything, I'm here for you."

Clara used her free hand to start twisting the seatbelt again. Dean almost wished he wasn't driving so he could hold onto both of her hands, to try to soothe all of her rather than just one part of her.

"How do you want me to respond to that?" Clara asked. "If I talk to you, you're just going to go off and beat him up. You're volatile, Dean. You always have been. You chainsawed a sofa, for crying out loud!"

"I'm working on it," Dean replied. He wasn't proud when he heard how defensive he was. He clenched his teeth together and looked away, out his window. He recognized the area, still unsure as to why he was coming here but deciding he wasn't quite ready to turn around. Not when he was getting so close to having a serious conversation with Clara. "I know I'm not perfect, Clara, but did you ever think, for one second, I would ever hurt you? Did I ever scare you because you thought something would happen to you?"

Clara tipped her head down, staring at her phone in her lap. She stopped twisting the seatbelt. Her hair fell into her face, her profile now masked by it.

"No."

The word was barely a breath, barely a caress, but he heard it. He didn't know why he felt relieved, but he did. If, even for a second, she was ever doubtful of him, he wouldn't know what to do. How to feel.

Dean pulled into a parking spot and Clara picked her eyes up.

"Where are we?" she asked.

Dean grinned. "You don't remember?" he chided. "Our spot."

## Chapter 11

THE BEACH.

Dean had taken her to the beach.

How fitting.

The sky was overcast, causing the ocean to look darker than it usually was. Instead of glittering and open, the water looked angry. Tumultuous. If anything, it seemed to resemble exactly how Clara was feeling. The waves sliced the shore in a biting, unforgivable manner. The back and forth between the water and the steady, stable shoreline was enough to calm the concern in Clara down. She let out a shaky breath, and then another. She had no idea how Dean remembered this place, how he knew she would react positively towards this.

But he did.

It really was their spot. They had spent so much of their time here when they were together. Clara could still feel the one bad sunburn she had received that summer. She remembered the feeling of Dean's hands on her back, rubbing lotion into her skin. It stung and felt amazing, a contradiction that constantly seemed to plague everything that had to do with Dean. Made Clara fall in love with him more because of his complexity and the new feelings he always seemed to bring out in her.

The relationship wasn't perfect by any stretch. They fought a lot over expectations that weren't being met.

And, Clara, realized, that was on her. She expected Dean to be some sort of Prince Charming wrapped up in the brutal force of an NHL badass.

But there was no prince underneath the jagged exterior.

Dean was exactly who he was. He was fierce and loyal. Every now and then, he could be sweet and romantic, but to expect that from him was only courting disappointment.

Maybe if she had known that when she was younger, maybe if she knew to accept him for exactly who he was, they would still be together now.

Maybe not. Dean was, after all, traded across the country, and Clara had been in college.

Maybe the distance and the time was enough for both of them to realize what they were missing.

Clara shook her head to herself. That wasn't something she needed to be thinking about. Not right now, after everything had happened with Bill. She would worry about any residual feelings later and focus on what needed to be done first.

Dean stepped out of the car and went to go pay for parking while Clara continued to wait in the car. She wasn't exactly dressed for the beach. She had on striped Calvin Klein pajama bottoms and an oversized t-shirt, with flip flops on her feet. Her hair was a tangled mess thanks to the fact that she couldn't brush it before she chose to leave, but at least she had the good sense to put on a bra. Especially since it looked colder than a beach was supposed to.

Though, if she was being honest, she loved this sort of weather, especially at the beach. It practically ensured that tourists would stay away, not wanting to chance time spent here was colder than their acceptable standards.

"You coming?" Dean stood by the side of the car, giving her a curious look. "The machine didn't spit me out a tab for the parking."

"You typed in a license plate?" Clara opened the door and stepped outside. The sun was high in the sky overhead, shining down on everything it could touch despite the clouds in its way as though it was determined to shine despite everyone blocking it from doing so. "You don't have to do that anymore. Put something on the dash, I mean. It logs your plate when you type it in."

"Oh." He stepped back as Clara turned and closed the door. "I guess a lot's change since I've been back, huh?" He glanced over at her. She wasn't sure how she was supposed to respond to that, so she didn't respond at all. He ask, "You ready?"

"Ready for what, exactly?" Clara asked, her voice hesitant. One of Dean's more positive qualities was that he was spontaneous. But that could also translate into not knowing what to expect. And Clara hated not knowing what to expect when it came to him.

The two began walking towards the beach. It felt weird not holding hands. They always held hands when they came here. It was just…it was natural, the way they did things. Not doing it was poignant, like they had to consciously make the choice not to do it.

And it didn't feel great.

"Some food," he said as though that much was obvious. Which it should have been. Dean had the biggest appetite of anyone she knew. How he managed to still look as fit as he did and eat what he ate was nothing short of a miracle. "And - hey, what happened to the Stuft Surfer?" He stopped walking, causing Clara to stop too.

Clara glanced over at the restaurant that was still under construction. "They're updating it, I think," she replied. "I don't know when it's going to be done, though. It's been under construction for a while." She looked over at Dean, eyes skimming across the concerned lines on his face. She reached out and gently took his hand in hers, giving it a little squeeze. That, alone, was enough for him to draw his attention back to her. "I miss it too."

Dean looked down at her for a long moment. Suddenly, Clara wasn't sure if she did the right thing. She tried to let Dean's hand go, but he wouldn't release his hold on her. "Really?" he asked, seemingly surprised. "You still come here."

"Don't let it go to your head," Clara said, a knowing look on her face. "I like the food. That is it."

"Okay." He did nothing to mask his doubt. "Since we can't eat, I guess that means we're going to have to do something else."

"Which is?" Clara couldn't help but wonder.

"Talk to me."

She gently pulled her hand away from Dean's in order to fiddle with the edge of the shirt she wore. She tried to twist it and slide the twisted material underneath the shirt, tying it without an actual knot. It gave her something to do with the excess of energy she had bundled up inside of her.

"About what?" she asked.

It was still April. Tourists didn't descend until May, around Memorial Day, so the boardwalk was somewhat empty. There was an elementary school on the beach with a playground in the sand. Besides a couple of toddlers, no one else was hanging out there. Some roller skaters skidded past the two, and an older couple walked their old beagle on the sand.

It was a nice day, even with the overcast. There was a gentle breeze that picked Clara's hair off of her shoulders. A bike rang its bell behind them and they stepped out of the way so the bike could maneuver around them.

"How you are?" he asked. "What have you been up to? I wrote you when you graduated school. Did you get my letter?"

"Surprisingly, yes." Clara felt her lips curl up. "I don't think my mom wanted me to have it. She was worried..." She let her voice trail off. She didn't want to say too much.

"Worried about what?" Dean prodded. At least he had the decency to be gentle about it.

"That it would break my heart all over again," Clara forced herself to finish. "To hear from you, I mean."

"Would it?" Dean asked. He turned his head so it was close to her, too close. His chin nearly grazed her shoulder, his lips nearly skimming over her cheekbone. But there was still a space between them, the space that protected the two from any distracting touching. "Would hearing from me have broken your heart?"

His voice was entirely too husky for a question like that. Clara didn't know how to answer because she didn't know how she would react. Instead, she sighed and turned away from him, looking at the narrow, three-story mansions that lined the board-walk. Some paid two grand a week just to rent a place here. Because of the limited space, barbecues were on rooftops and balconies were nonexistent. It bothered Clara how many of the houses were filled with glass. It was so easy to look inside and see how someone lived. There was no privacy living right on the beach, even for a week.

"Why did you take me here?" Clara asked him. She crossed her arms over her chest. The breeze turned colder and she felt her arms burst into goosebumps. Even though her hair had dried, there was a chill that slid down her spine. She stopped walking and a skateboarder nearly ran into her. She didn't even care. Her focus was on Dean.

"Honestly, I don't know." The way his blue eyes gleamed, Clara could tell he was being serious. He didn't look amused, the way he usually was about everything. Now, he looked pensive, maybe even slightly unsure, which was typically how Dean acted even if he felt otherwise. "I knew I had to get you away from Bill. I didn't want you to think I was taking advantage of the situation and I didn't want to make you feel uncomfortable by taking you back to my place. So I took you here." He looked away from her, his eyes going over to the water. Without warning, he wrapped his arm around her waist and brought her across the cement sidewalk until they reached the sand. Now, they could talk without worrying about anyone bumping into them. "You always looked so peaceful here. That time you got into that huge fight with your mom when she found out we were dating, we came here at midnight. We weren't supposed to be out so late but the cop who caught us was a hockey fan and he gave us a warning. You remember that?"

Clara chuckled in spite of herself. Her eyes were focused on the horizon but she could feel Dean's arm still hanging onto her waist. She didn't want to remove it from her, even if she should. It managed to take that chill from before and quell it with warmth.

"How could I forget?" she asked. "It was the only time in my life where I thought my mom was going to hit me."

"How is your mom?" Dean asked. He sounded like he genuinely wanted to know.

"You know how she is, though she has calmed down a bit," Clara said. She removed her flip flops and buried her bare feet in the cool sand, feeling herself relax even further. "I guess tempers do calm down with age."

Dean snorted, giving her a disbelieving look. "I highly doubt that," he said.

"She was glad when we broke up," Clara admitted. She walked further towards the ocean, Dean walking right beside her and keeping up with no effort. "But she didn't like who I was when I was getting over you. I did, though, eventually. And now I have my own business. She liked Bill —"

"Liked?" Dean asked, turning his head. Clara let him catch eyes with her, her hair pushing against her face as though the red locks could magically go through instead of around. "Are you saying Ms. Daniels doesn't like him anymore?"

Clara snorted, shaking her head. His arm was still wrapped around her waist and she couldn't help but let herself imagine what this might be like if they weren't awkward puzzle pieces, trying to fit together, unsure if they would again. But he made her feel warm. He made her feel taken care of. And that was something Bill hadn't provided. Maybe that meant something. Maybe now wasn't the time to think about it.

"My mom changes her mind about people all the time," she reminded him. She started burying her right foot in the sand, letting the sand fall on her foot before lifting her foot up and letting the sand fall away. "Except you." She picked her head up and shot him a grin. "She never came around to liking you."

"I'm honored," he said flatly. He stepped in front of her, cutting off her view of the ocean. "Tell me, Clara. Was it the first time he laid his hands on you? I get that you don't want to talk about it. I respect it. But –"

"You think I would go back to someone who hit me?" Clara asked.

"Are you?" Dean squeezed her side before dropping his hand. "Are you going back to him, Clara? Did he hit you? Why?" He pressed his lips together before taking a step back and shaking his head. "I'm sorry. I shouldn't... I'm over-whelming you. It's none of my business. But I want to know what you're thinking. I want to know how you feel. I want to know how I can help. I want to know everything. I feel like I'm standing to the side, watching something happen to you that I have no control over. And I don't know how I can make it better, and that's all I want to do."

Clara took in a deep breath, the salt-tainted wind tickling her nose.

"What happened was the first time," she said slowly, tilting her head so her hair wouldn't hit her face anymore. She squinted, trying to position herself so he blocked the sun from glaring down at her. "He never came home last night. Didn't text me. I woke up alone so I went to shower. He came in and saw my phone and decided to go through my messages."

"He doesn't trust you?" Dean asked.

"We all do crazy things," she said. "I used to do that to you all the time."

"I didn't care," he replied with a shrug. "I wasn't keeping anything from you."

"Yeah, but regardless, it isn't my business." She huffed out a sigh and looked back at the water from over Dean's broad shoulder.

"So, what, you're defending what he did?" Clara could tell Dean was trying to keep his voice civil but he was having a difficult time doing so. "Since you did it to me, it's okay for him to do it to you?"

"That's not what I'm saying at all," she insisted. "Bill saw the texts from you. He saw your texts and it pissed him off. You pissed him off." She shook her head. "Regardless of the fight I had with him about not believing me about us, what I did... our texts didn't exactly help things. If I had seen those texts on his phone —"

"Are you kidding me, Clara?" Dean asked. He hadn't raised his voice but it was sharp and it forced Clara to snap her eyes back to his. "We are —"

"What? Friends?" She stepped out of his grip and walked around him. She reached down and grabbed the material of her pajama pants and hiked them up so they bunched around her knees. She kicked off her flip flops before heading straight into the water. The sand was mud and slopped up between her toes. The cool ocean rinsed the mud away except those grains that were stuck on her skin. "What are we, Dean? Because we definitely aren't friends."

"I don't know what you want me to say to that." Dean followed her to the water but he didn't remove his shoes. The water pushed against him and Clara knew his socks were now damp with salt water but Dean didn't seem to care. "I don't know what label you want to give it to make you more comfortable with it. All I know is that I still dream about you. I can still hear your voice in my head. I can still feel your body in my hands."

Clara felt her hands shake with each word he spoke. She snapped them into fists and wished she had pockets to shove them in. She didn't want him to see. She didn't want him to know that he still had an effect on her as well.

"You're everything, Clara," Dean continued, taking a step towards her. "You always been. You will always be. Someone hurting you, however minuscule it may be, infuriates me. Because I know I hurt you and I would give anything - *anything* - to take back what I did to you."

"What are you saying?" Clara asked.

But she knew.

She knew.

Without warning, Dean grabbed her face and crashed lips onto hers.

# Chapter 12

THE LAST THING Dean expected was to kiss her. But God, he needed this. He needed this more than he realized. He needed this like women needed chocolate and men needed the remote. He needed to have his lips on Clara's, to breathe her in, to remind himself what she tasted like - because, goddammit, nobody else tasted the exact same way she did.

She belonged to him. It was sexist and demeaning and not fair to her, but that was how he felt. She was his in every sense of the word - her mind, her body, her spirit.

His.

She was all his.

And now that he had had her back, it was like his whole fucking world had shifted again and it was just her and him. It was like the pieces fell back into place, like everything was right in the world once more.

He could feel the gentle sea breeze nip his neck and cause the hairs on his skin to stand straight up. He could hear the cawing of sea gulls a distance away and the waves crashing to the shore before sliding back out to sea once more. Laughter pierced the sky; the elementary school was probably on recess and kids were playing on the playground. It was the perfect sound that represented how he felt on the inside. Hell, if he were a kid, he'd be giggling right now too.

But none of that mattered. Not when his lips were on Clara's and she was letting him kiss her like she still belonged to him after all of these years.

Which she did.

But the fact that she was acknowledging it, that she was willing to let this happen, was more than he could hope for.

Dean prided himself on being both experienced and knowledgeable when it came to pleasing a partner. He had a reputation that he made sure to uphold, no matter who was in his bed or on the receiving end of something quick and meaningless. It amazed him how quickly someone like Clara could bring him to his knees, could make him question everything he thought he once knew about what it meant to please a woman. His prowess was suddenly not natural and he had to remember what to do to make sure she approved of the kiss, to have it sear into her brain like a goddamn tattoo.

He never doubted himself. Even now, he knew he was giving her the best of him. But that didn't necessarily mean she wanted it.

Sure, she was kissing him back. Now.

But he wanted her for more than just a moment.

He wanted her for life. He wouldn't accept anything less. But that didn't mean she wanted him back in the same way.

*You're worrying about this fucking now? Fucking enjoy the moment, you prick.*

Slowly, Clara slid her hands up Dean's chest before locking her wrists behind his neck, drawing him down, closer to her. Dean breathed her in, a hint of something flowery consuming her and making him fall even harder than before. He didn't remember that scent from when they were first together. Whether it was new, whether it was old, it didn't matter. It consumed him, just like everything else about her did. Whatever the hell it was, it was his new favorite scent because it was her. It was all her. And if he ever smelled it somewhere else, he would always associate it with her.

Dean slid his tongue along her bottom lip. He knew she loved when he did that - at least, she had, back when they had been together. It always made her open her mouth for him, as if by accident. Even if she didn't want to. Even if she was trying to fight for dominance.

This time, instead of opening her mouth, her own tongue met his and they battled, fighting for that dominance. He grinned through the kiss. He should have predicted she would fight with him every step of the way. He fucking adored her for it.

Dean felt himself get hard, kissing her like this. He typically had better control over himself but he felt like he was some kind of teenage boy and she was the hot book nerd he lusted after but could never win.

His hands tightened their grip on her - one hand cupped her hip, the other was buried in her hair, fisting the back of her head so he had some kind of control over her. He tried to tilt his pelvis back, away from her. He wanted to ensure this kiss lasted, and he wasn't sure how she'd react if she knew he was causing her body to react in a certain way. He didn't want to scare her off, didn't want to ruin this so soon after it started. He also didn't want her to think she had such power over him, even if she did. It would be like stripping himself open and letting her see into his deepest, darkest secrets, letting her see his weakness even if maybe she could exploit it. He didn't want that, and yet, he couldn't help himself. It was as though she had that power over him, and there was nothing he could do about it.

In truth, he didn't want to do anything about it.

He wanted it even more.

He wanted to bare himself to her and have her do the same for him.

Clara's tongue was much fiercer than he remembered. He grunted. He was becoming more and more affected by the fact that she was willing to put up a fight with him, that she wouldn't so easily let him simply kiss her. Her fingers started tugging at his hair and he gently bit her bottom lip, eliciting a groan from her.

Dean froze.

That sound.

If he thought he was hard before, the sound that came out of her mouth caused him to throb with desire. He had forgotten that sound, but hearing it made all of the memories he buried, he tried to forget with booze and other women, pop back up, eager to take flight. It was like the dam had been destroyed and a torrent of memories surrounded him, refusing to let him go. He was done for. He was drowning in her.

He needed to hear it again and again. He needed to be the only one to elicit that sound from her. His grip on her tightened like he needed to leave his mark on her, needed to sear himself into her skin so she would remember this, remember *him*, and everything they felt when they were together.

And then, they both had to come up for air.

Fuck.

He had never hated having to breathe before until this moment.

Fucking hell, they had to take a breath. Dean refused to release his hold on her, afraid that if he did, she might step away and realize that this wasn't something she wanted to do, at least not with him. Afraid she might realize that they weren't together, that this wasn't their world, that she could leave him right now and never have to see him again.

That would utterly fucking break him.

If that was what she really wanted, he didn't want her to force herself to be with him. But he also didn't want her to be afraid of being with him either. He knew things last time didn't end the way either of them wanted, but maybe…maybe they had a chance to do it all over again. Maybe they could do better, *be* better, together.

He sucked in the fresh air as best as he could without being desperate. His eyes were on her, refusing to even let her out of his sight. He didn't want her to leave. But he didn't want her to stay because she felt she had to. He wasn't sure what he wanted. He didn't know what this meant. Were they together? Were they suddenly back on after years of being off? Could things really go back to the way they were? Was that what he wanted? Was that what she wanted? What *did* she want when it came to Dean anyway?

There were too many fucking questions, questions he didn't have the answer to. Which meant, he wasn't fucking sure what the hell to do about it.

"Well." He needed to say something. Maybe he'd think of something the more he talked.

Heh.

Fat chance.

Usually, he had to stick his foot in his mouth the majority of the fucking time.

"Yeah."

He couldn't tell if she actually said anything. The word was airy and light, like she didn't have breath to speak.

Dean didn't know where to go from there. His mind was searching for more - something more to say, something more to do, something to keep this moment going and turn it into more than just catching a breath.

Their eyes clashed. He used to be able to red those dark orbs. Now...

He still could.

Fuck, he still could.

And she wanted this just as much as he did.

And then, Clara surprised him by reaching back up and pulling him down again. His lips found hers, her fingers were in his hair, his hands were on her waist, and everything was right. Everything felt right. And he wanted more of this.

*More, more, more.*

One word, chanting in his head, like a mantra, over and over again.

"I can't —"

The words ripped from his mouth when they were forced to breathe again. His hair was completely messy and askew. His shirt was wrinkled. He was a mess and he didn't give a shit.

"We need to go somewhere," she said.

Dean couldn't tell if she had just read his mind or if she was feeling the same way as before. Regardless, he felt himself nodding in agreement.

Yes, wherever the hell she wanted to go. He would follow her to the ends of the earth, to the gates of Hell, wherever the fuck she wanted to go, he would follow her like a fucking puppy.

He didn't even care if that made him into a pussy. He'd fucking take whatever scraps she fed him and then thank her for it.

"Yes," he agreed. "Yes, you're right."

The corner of Clara's lip ticked up. "Wow," she murmured. "I never thought I'd ever hear you say that."

"What?"

"That I'm right about something."

"You were right about a lot of things," he said, shifting his weight. "I just didn't like to admit when I was wrong." Clara opened her mouth, ready to respond, but Dean jumped in. "Just shut up. Let's go back to my place."

He grabbed her hand and led her away from the beach. She barely had enough time to grab her flip flops before they were forgotten in the sand. His toes started to get buried by sand drying on his skin but he didn't care. All that mattered was getting Clara back to his place and —

And then what? Would she really jump right back into bed with him? Or was this just a one-time thing? Was this really the time to be thinking about something like this? She had just been through an ordeal. Something with heavy consequences. He didn't want to take advantage of her, but truth be told, he still didn't know what he wanted when it came to Clara.

"What are you thinking?" Clara squeezed his hand and looked up at him with her big brown eyes. "You're too quiet. Your brain must be going off."

He grinned down at her but his heart wasn't in it. "Honestly, Clara, I want to go back to my place with you and finally be with you again, but I want to make sure that's something you want," he admitted. His voice was strained and he shoved his free hand in the pocket of his leather jacket or else he would find himself fiddling with things, like belt loops and fingers. He had never been good at discussing serious things like the future but there was something in him that was compelled to do that - at least, for Clara. "I know you've been through a lot the past few hours. I just - I don't want you to be with me if you don't want to be with me."

The corners of Clara's lips tilted up into a small, mischievous grin. He could tell by the glint in her eye that she wasn't mocking him or laughing at him.

"I appreciate that, Dean." She tugged on his hand so they stopped walking once they were near the parking lot. "Honestly, I didn't expect that coming from you. I mean, I know you're considerate, when you want to be. But I'm sure you know you have a reputation -"

"It's bullshit." He didn't even flinch as he said it. In fact, he pulled his hand from his pocket so he could cup Clara's face in his palm. "Everything is bullshit. Did I sleep with women after I left? Yes. But they're nothing. Nothing compared to you. You have to know that."

"You didn't need to tell me that, Dean," Clara said. Her eyes were serious. "What happened after me -"

"I never - not while we were together."

She smiled, and he could see a reflection of the clouds in her eyes. "I never thought you did," she said. "You were a pain in my ass, but I knew you'd never cheat on me."

For whatever reason, the fact that Clara knew this without a doubt made Dean fill with warmth and relief. For so long, he had been worried that Clara would assume he cheated on her, especially since the news outlets had reported, at the time, that she (unknown to the media) broke up with him because he couldn't keep it in his pants. And that much was true, but only with Clara. He was crazy about her in every possible way.

He ducked his head and gave her a lingering kiss on her lips. Clara tensed underneath it, and he immediately pulled back, his eyes searching hers.

"Dean," she breathed out. They were so close, their foreheads were nearly touching. A rollerblader dodged them, and a biker yelled at them, until Dean dragged Clara out of the sidewalk and closer to the small parking lot on Fifteenth Street. "What happened between us... it broke my heart. I knew I'd eventually move on but I wouldn't say I'm over it. I didn't think we ever got the closure we deserved. And if we go back to your place..." He could tell she was trying to read his eyes. He didn't know what she saw but he hoped she saw something in them that would help her trust him more. "I never really stopped loving you, Dean. And I'm sorry. I don't mean to put this on you. I know you're in the last series of the season and you guys are so close to winning the Stanley Cup. But I just want to be honest with you. We've always been honest with each other and I don't want that to change, regardless of what we do."

Dean was breathing hard. He swallowed, his throat suddenly dry. He dropped his hand from her face, letting it smack his thigh. He didn't even notice.

"I don't give a shit about the Cup," he managed to get out.

A skeptical brow sprang up on Clara's face and she crossed her arms over her chest, giving Dean an expectant look. The wind finally calmed down so her hair wasn't blowing in her face. He wanted to kiss her again, even though her lips looked decidedly bruised.

"I mean, I do, but when it comes to you..." He let his voice trail off. He hated this. He hated trying to be both romantic and honest because words never came out the way he wanted them to. "I want to do right by you, Clara. If you want me to marry you, I'd fly you to Vegas. If you want me to never bother you again, it would fucking break my heart, but I would figure out how to do that. I'm crazy about you. I want you. When you left that night, I was absolutely livid. I broke all of my mother's china and she still hasn't forgiven me - or you - for it. I ruined my sofa because it smelled like you, because I couldn't sit on it without being reminded of you. And now that I'm here, with you, I don't want to let you go, but I don't want to lead you on. I don't know the right answer. I don't know what I want. But I want you. In whatever way you want to give me."

Clara was silent for a long moment before a smile spread across her face. "Dean," she murmured, making his heart skip. "Take me to your place."

## Chapter 13

CLARA HAD NEVER BEEN to Dean's new place before - and for good reason. Besides the fact that there was no reason for her to be there in the first place, she didn't want to see it, didn't even want to know where it was located. She didn't trust herself around him - and for good reason. Even now, she felt conflicting emotions swirling inside of her. Maybe if the whole thing with Bill hadn't happened, maybe if she was massively in love with him the way she thought she had been, this would be easier. Being around Dean, even coming to his home, would be easier. As it was, she knew the tension between them, the issues she hadn't realized they had, brought up doubt.

Doubt about everything.

About what she wanted.

About who she wanted to be with.

After what Bill did, she knew she was getting ready to leave him. But that didn't mean she was ready to be with Dean.

And yet, the thought of that wasn't as bad as she thought it would be.

She blew out a breath and tried to focus on her surroundings. She wasn't surprised to see the house was large and over the top, much like Dean Morgan himself. It was a single-story, five bedroom home that sat on the cliffs overlooking the ocean, deep in the heart of Corona Del Mar. Technically speaking, CDM was part of Newport Beach but there was a divide between Newport and CDM, both financially and in the people who occupied both places. Unless you made multi-millions every year, you probably lived in a big house on a plot of land where parking absolutely sucked because tourists refused to pay for parking at the beach and, instead, chose to fill the neighborhood communities with their parked cars, making it impossible for actual CDM residents to find parking in front of their own houses. However, there was a part of CDM that wasn't too clogged up, either because it was in a community that restricted access to it via a gate or because there was only direct access to the beach through a residential home.

Dean lived in the latter. It shouldn't surprise Clara. Because he didn't really have family save for a mother who lived up north and who rarely talked to him, the money he made as a professional athlete was invested in property rather than anything else. The Dean she remembered liked luxury cars, but he didn't need tons of them. He preferred his Jaguar, and, if Clara had to guess, probably only had one of them tucked away in his garage, next to his precious BMW.

Although, she couldn't help but wonder why he felt he needed a house as big as this when it was only him. Who was he buying this for? What was he trying to prove?

Part of her wanted to ask him, and maybe she would have, if they were still together, still close enough where she felt as though she could ask him anything.

But that wasn't them any more.

The realization hit Clara like a slap in the face, even though she had known this for a while. The knots in her stomach tightened, twisting her insides. She didn't like that she wasn't close with Dean anymore. She wanted to change that.

But changing that meant being with Dean, with trusting him again, and she wasn't sure she was ready to do that either.

"I see you're intent on settling down here after retirement," Clara said as he pulled the SUV into his garage.

One glance to her right, and she found she was correct, at least about the cars. A total of three cars, a Jaguar, a BMW, and this Chevy Tahoe.

"Retirement?" Dean asked. "What's that?"

Clara exited the car with a small smirk on her face. Typical Dean. The guy would play until he died, if he could.

He led her through the garage and into the house. There was a narrow hallway with wooden floors. To her right, there was a small room with a washer and dryer, and two baskets of overflowing clothes that probably included his sweat-filled workout gear. Clara shouldn't be surprised. Dean always hated the laundry. She was surprised not to see some sexy maid, cleaning his house so he didn't have to, flouncing around in some sexy outfit. Relief flooded through her but she pushed it away, and instead, focused her attention on his home once more.

The hallway was filled with picture of him and his team-mates, some on the ice during a game, while others were at community and other nonprofit events.

She stepped into the living room with a leather couch shaped like an L, a large glass coffee table with various sports magazines sprawled across the surface, and a sixty-four inch 4K television hanging above a banister and a fireplace. There were a couple more pictures in the stairwell, these more intimate than his hockey ones. A couple were of Dean when he was a kid, one of him and his mom at his college graduation, and then finally, a black and white photo of Clara herself at the beach. Her back faced the camera and she turned her head to the camera - to Dean - an impish smile on her face.

"I remember that day," Clara murmured before she could stop herself. She grabbed the picture in her hand, smiling. In all honesty, she couldn't believe he actually kept it. It meant that every time he looked at it, he would think of her.

Her heart clenched. She wasn't sure what to do with that information.

"I have to tell people your picture is the one that came with the frame," he said in a rough voice.

Suddenly, it was difficult for Clara to swallow. Her throat had gone dry and she was forced to set the picture back on the bannister. She wanted to ask why she needed to tell anyone anything in the first place, but she bit the tip of her tongue in order to restrain herself. They were treading into dangerous territory, and she didn't want to risk it.

She didn't *think* she wanted to risk it.

Dean came up behind her and snaked his arms around her waist so her back hit his broad chest. Clara let out a shaky breath. She should pull away. She wasn't ready for this. And yet, nothing in her body moved. She was as rigid as a stone. Because she knew, deep down, that she wanted this. He leaned his head down until his lips found her neck. She stiffened under his touch, but her pulse jumped against her throat.

She knew he could feel her tense. She knew he could feel her hesitation.

But he didn't stop.

Maybe that should have been a red flag. Maybe that should have been enough to tell herself that this wasn't going the way she wanted it to.

But her body…

Her goddamn traitorous body…

It was like it never forgot anything he had done to her. Never forgot, and craved it all the more.

She hated herself for being unable to pull away, to maintain a level-head, a clear distance. But she couldn't. There was no need to fight it. She couldn't do that even if she tried.

And the truth of the matter was, she didn't want to.

Not anymore.

His grip on her hips tightened and he flicked his tongue against the most sensitive part of her throat. He still remembered. She shouldn't have been surprised, but she was. She let out a little gasp. Her eyebrows shot up but her eyes rolled closed and the hard surface that she tried to project around him started to melt away. She pushed against him in that way she knew he liked, her pulse tapping furiously in her throat, waiting to be consumed by him the same way her flesh was.

"You like this?" he asked, his voice a low growl, dancing across her skin. She opened her mouth to respond but no sound came out. "Don't answer that, I know you do. You've always liked this."

Clara let out a shaky breath as she felt his teeth start to nibble on her skin.

"You taste so damn good, Clara. *Fuck*."

God, how he said her name. It always shot little lightning bolts straight to her pelvis. It always caused goosebumps to break out across her skin. It caused shivers to slide down her spine and her folds to moisten with desire. It was like a spell he cast to put her under his command; she would do anything when he said her name like that.

He was her weakness. He would always be her weakness.

His hands began to play with the hemline of her shirt. Each time his finger caressed the soft skin just underneath her stomach, she let out a small, nearly inaudible moan. Her head hit his shoulder and she tilted her head away, just enough, giving him even more access to her throat, like prey finally surrendering to its death.

Dean could hear it, though. She knew he could. He might pretend not to understand. He might pretend he didn't listen. But he picked up on a lot more than he was given credit for.

Dean slowly pulled her shirt over her head and tossed it behind him so it landed carelessly on the floor. She was left in a bra and pajama pants. Dean had to move more of it out of the way as his lips descended even further until they reached her shoulder. His hands pressed flat against her stomach and slowly traced her curves until they reached her lacy bra. Suddenly, they vanished. Judging by the pressure on her back, she knew he was fiddling with unhooking her bra. Clara had to bite back a smile. Dean has so much skill in practically every area of life; it would make sense this was the only thing that didn't come easy to him.

After a few more minutes, he finally unfastened the hooks, growling and cursing under his breath as he did so. Gently, he removed each strap from her arms and released his hold on the bra so it fell in front of her, on the marble tile just before the fireplace.

His hands came up and clutched her breasts from behind. Her head fell back against his collarbone and she pushed her chest out, giving him better access to her breasts.

"I know how you want it," he whispered in her ear, causing her to get more goosebumps.

Her nipples marbled underneath his touch so quickly, Clara was almost embarrassed. But it felt too good to do anything else, and there was no way in hell she was stopping him.

"Tell me to stop." His teeth grazed her neck. "Tell me to stop and I will."

Was he crazy? Why would he think she would ever want him to stop?

"Please," she whimpered. "Don't stop."

He growled. She could feel his hardness press against her and she took in a quick breath, anticipating him turning her around and bending her over the couch.

Before they broke up, their relationship was filled with passion - fucking everywhere, every way. There was intimacy behind it, but that usually took a backseat to the lust.

And that was okay.

Looking back, Clara blushed just remembering how she was completely incapable of keeping her hands to herself. Despite the fact that nine years had passed, she still expected the same urgency between them, especially since they hadn't spoken, hadn't figured out what they were, what kind of relationship this was.

Without warning, Dean grabbed her and threw her over his shoulder like she was a sack of ice - easy for him to carry. Instead of leading her to the couch as she expected, he slowly made his way to what Clara assumed was his bedroom.

There was no time to take in his room. All she could see were white, navy, and red colors - very nautical in design. Her heart pounded. She loved nautical design, still did. She remembered decorating his apartment similarly before he left for Florida. She wondered if he liked it so much he kept the idea, or if there was more to it than just that. If it had to do with her, with being reminded of her, like she never left him even if he left her.

He gently placed her on the bed so she was on her back. His hungry eyes found hers and he did not blink, did not look away, as he slowly peeled off her pants and then her underwear.

He was still too dressed for the occasion. Clara would be lying if she said she didn't feel vulnerable under his gaze. They knew each other so well, and yet, there was still that nervousness that bubbled up in her stomach, like a shaken up soda can.

"Goddamn, if you don't look as beautiful as ever," he muttered in a husky voice.

He reached behind him to tug up his shirt.

Clara immediately sat up. Her face was still reeling from the gentle blush that had caressed her cheeks, thanks to Dean's proclamation of her beauty. She coiled her arms around his waist, pulling her to him. His abs looked more defined than she remembered, sharp, like a washboard. She couldn't stop herself from running her fingers over the edges. Dean flinched under her touch, and she realized just how much power over him she held. She kissed his stomach once, then twice. His hand found the back of her head and he tightened his grip.

He wanted to be in control. She let him.

Gently, he pushed her back so she was lying down. His hands fumbled for his jeans and it wasn't long before he got rid of them and then his boxer briefs. He leaned over her and grabbed a condom from the nightstand. She was grateful he remembered. She probably wouldn't have said anything if he hadn't slipped the condom on.

He leaned over her, completely naked, his cock erect and waiting. His eyes feasted on her body and she could not help but squirm slightly underneath his gaze.

"You're a goddamn masterpiece, Clara." His eyes were on hers when he said the words, not her breasts or her pelvis or her soft stomach. Her eyes. "God, I've missed you. I've missed this."

He crawled over her and she shuddered. Just seeing him on top of her, seeing him above her, his powerful arms pinning her between them so she couldn't escape even if she wanted to.

When he slid into her - slowly, gently - she felt herself sigh. Not because she was tired. Not because she was bored or considered this a chore. But because this felt right. Because this felt the way it always had. It felt like to pieces of a puzzle fitting perfectly together, bringing each other pleasure simply by connecting.

He let out a grunt, his eyes snapping shut, and he paused. It appeared as though he didn't trust himself to continue on. Clara could hear him muttering to himself but she was so enraptured that she couldn't hear him clearly.

But that only lasted so long.

His hands gripped her hips and he started thrusting into her hard. He didn't even ask as he slid his hand between their bodies and started to dance his fingers across her clit.

She let out a moan, tightening her thighs. Her ankles locked around his back and her fingers tugged at his hair.

It was just like old times, only better. They both had experience. They both missed each other. They both craved each other just like they had before. The best part was that they still remembered each other. She knew his body. She knew he liked when she ran her fingers down his back and she loved when he teased her nipples.

It wasn't long before she felt her body start to build up tension. She was going to come. Her breathing turned ragged.

She tried to get the words out but she couldn't. She wanted him to know but all she could muster was his name - and she couldn't even be certain that he heard that.

She crashed around him. She felt him stiffen inside of her and then he continued to thrust, letting out a long, low moan.

Clara somehow felt both energized and exhausted. Her brain was fuzzy. He collapsed on top of her and she welcomed him with open arms. She didn't know much. She didn't know what this was. But she knew she didn't want to be anywhere else but here with Dean right now.

# Chapter 14

DEAN COULDN'T SLEEP. His whole routine was off now, thanks to the woman wrapped in his arms. She felt exactly the same, but there was something different about her, something new and exciting. He wanted to feel her like that, wrap himself up in it, never forget what it felt like. It was bliss, at first, something he didn't particularly worry about. This was what he wanted. Clara was here. They had just had the best sex of his life, in his bed, and now she was here with him, sleeping softly in his arms. She still drooled too. He couldn't help but grin at the sight, and pushed an errant strand of red hair out of her peaceful face. She sighed in contentment, shifting in her sleep. She didn't wake up though. Everything about him squeezed. He loved her.

Shit, he still loved her like it was six years ago. Like those feelings never went away.

And maybe they hadn't. Maybe all he had done was treat them like they were a television and he muted them so he could ignore the way they made him feel, didn't have to listen to how he ruined everything.

Currently, they were on full blast, ringing in his ears,

vibrating throughout his entire body. Hell, if he closed his eyes, he could feel like his bed shook with them.

But now what?

With those feelings so pressing, he couldn't deny them. Not that he had before, but it was easier to ignore, to distract himself with other things. But now that they shook him to his very core, he knew he needed to figure out what to do about them.

Did he confess his love for her? Because he did love her. That much was certain. And he had no problem admitting it to her, or even to himself. The timing - was it right? Should he wait until after the finals?

He didn't give a shit about Bill, especially after the way that fucker treated her, but maybe she still did. And even though it went against every fiber in his being, he wanted to make sure she was ready to hear Dean confess his feelings because he definitely didn't want to fuck this up again. Now that he had Clara, now that there was a good possibility they could stay together, there was no way he was going to risk giving it up because he couldn't control his mouth or he acted selfishly.

It had to be about *her*. It had to.

Dean always grabbed breakfast after morning skate before coming home and watching a couple of hours of mindless television. It helped to get his mind off of hockey temporarily, and *The Real Housewives of Atlanta* usually helped him do that. Then, he would go to Ma's, a hole-in-the-wall Italian place south on PCH, near Balboa, and get a large plate of her homemade spaghetti with meat sauce. He would always get it to go, he would eat, and then he would nap, before he was expected to start getting ready.

He never had to worry about sex before. Back in Florida, he made the playoffs four times during his tenure with them. He never had sex on game days, though it wasn't as though that had been planned. Typically, he focused solely on hockey during game days. In all honesty, he didn't notice other girls when he was so primarily focused on the task at hand. Off days, he partied, but not the way he usually did. He made sure he was disciplined in whatever capacity he could be during the playoffs.

Technically speaking, today wasn't a game day. But sex never happened during the afternoon. It only happened at night. And sex had never been with Clara. Never with the one he really wanted it to be with.

Now that it had...

Was he fucked in more ways than one? His whole game plan was out the window now. She had thrown a wrench into it, and he couldn't even be mad about it. He wanted this to happen, but the timing...

Fuck the timing. He would take it in whatever way he could get it. If it meant he got Clara, he would handle everything else.

Dean pulled Clara closer to his body, doing his best not to wake her. He wanted her to sleep as much as she could. After what had happened to her...

He couldn't even finish the thought. He was lucky Clara had pulled him away. He had been ready to beat Bill to a bloody pulp.

Was it wrong he didn't even blink an eye at inflicting that much pain in one human being? Not only that, but he was willing to risk everything - the Stanley Cup Finals - to beat the shit out of someone. Dean didn't care that this person was a fan. Hell, he didn't give a shit about who Bill was. He didn't care that there was a good chance Bill would press charges and he'd probably either go to jail for assault or have to pay some kind of fine. And that was before Bill probably took him to civil court and sued him for bitch-ass damages. He didn't give a shit about any of that.

Then again, Clara had always been his exception. He would do anything for her - and that scared him shitless. He didn't do anything for anyone, unless it was his team.

Dean's stomach growled, interrupting his thoughts. He quickly looked over at Clara, wondering if she had been disturbed by his incessant stomach. When he still heard her purring evenly, he relaxed. However, he knew Clara had an appetite - especially after a sex nap - and she would not be in a good mood if she didn't get food in her system when she woke up. There was still food in his cupboards and in his fridge he could use to cook. He couldn't even remember the last time he actually cooked - unless a bagel counted, and he didn't think it did.

He sighed, resting his eyes on her once again. He gently traced the outline of her body, trying to memorize her shape, trying to memorize everything about her. He wanted to hold onto this moment for as long as he possibly could, knowing there was a good chance he would have to let it go. Knowing there was a chance that she didn't want him the way he wanted her.

Slowly, he disentangled from her and slid out of his bed. The cool air smacked him like a sucker punch to the gut. He pulled on his sweatpants and nothing else before heading for the door. When he reached the frame, he glanced back at Clara and felt himself grin.

Regardless of what was going to happen between them at this point, even if she broke his heart and went back to that asshole, or even broke up with that asshole and wanted nothing to do with him, it was worth it. Even if his day was completely discombobulated thanks to the new turn of events, it was worth it. Anything that had to do with Clara was always worth it.

He headed down the stairs and went straight to his kitchen. From the corner of his eye, he noticed the discarded bra and the shirt that Dean had pulled off of her body. He felt his cock stirring at the sight. The fact that they were Clara's turned him on. He hadn't had that reaction before with anyone else. It was like he could imagine that she lived with him, that she still belonged to him in a way she could never belong to anyone else. And he wanted to hold onto that feeling for as long as possible.

For the next fifteen minutes, Dean scoured through his walk-in cabinets, looking for something that was both edible and not toast, bagels, cereal, or oatmeal. When he came up with nothing, he tried the fridge. He wasn't cable to find anything solid. As such, he decided it might be best to order out. Then, his eyes caught sight of eggs and shredded cheese and grinned.

Back when they used to date, Clara was obsessed with his omelets. He always gave her extra cheese. At the time, she had been a vegetarian, so he would chop up onions and peppers and make sure there was a healthy mixture of the vegetables. One time, he added a hint of jalapeño and it did wonders to the food. He glanced around his produce section. He definitely had onions and had green pepper but it didn't look like he had any jalapeño. He had stopped buying it at the grocery store. It reminded him too much of Clara and he didn't want to be reminded of her.

He placed his ingredients on the marble countertop and bent down to grab a pan. He turned on the stove and started to let the pan heat up while he chopped up the vegetables. The strong scent caused his stomach rumble, eagerly anticipating tasting his own creation.

"Alexa," he said to the Amazon Dot sitting on his microwave, "play Bon Jovi."

Eighties music filled his kitchen and he grinned, moving around the kitchen. Dean wasn't a dancer. He liked to move his body on the ice, he liked to move his body during sex. He didn't really see the point in moving his body to music, even good music like Bon Jovi. But he couldn't help himself. Not now.

He was…happy.

For no reason, other than something good had happened to him. And he wanted to keep that feeling going. He wanted to continue to feel this way because, in all honesty, he hadn't felt like this in so long.

"'*Wanted: Dead or Alive*,'" a voice said from the stairway. "Why am I not surprised?"

Dean glanced up and had to do a double-take. There was

Clara, in one of his t-shirts and boxers, hair all mussed because of the sex, looking tired and content. He smiled.

"Hello."

She lifted her nose up in the air, making her way into the kitchen as if she owned the place. She'd never set foot into his home until a few hours ago, and yet, it felt right, having her here. She fit.

"Are you making –" She turned to him with a wide grin on her face. "The Morgan Special!"

"The Morgan Special was what I gave you a few hours ago," Dean drawled, giving her a wink. Clara rolled her eyes but smiled as she took a seat at the bar.

"Anything I can help you with while you cook?" she asked, resting her chin in her palm. Her eyes were on him as he continued to chop up the peppers and he suddenly felt shy, unsure how to handle her piercing stare.

"Just sit there and salivate," he said.

The music continued to hang in the room. From the corner of his eye, he saw Clara mouthing the words to the song. She loved Bon Jovi nearly as much as he did and knew the words to all their major songs - and she wasn't afraid to sing them. She actually didn't sound half-bad and he would always try to get her to do karaoke but she claimed she was too shy.

Right.

It took him fifteen more minutes before he had a plate of omelets in front of her, sprinkled with lots and lots of cheese. Clara didn't wait for permission. She took the fork he offered her and dug in.

"You are going to share, aren't you?" he teased, walking around the bar to sit next to her. He reached out with his own fork in order to try and claim a piece of the omelet for himself.

"Share? Not in my vocabulary." Her eyes sparkled but she leaned away from him in order to give him better access to the plate.

"I remember that," Dean said. "I also remember you

preferred a healthy amount of cheese on your food. I can see that that hasn't changed."

Clara grinned but couldn't speak right that second, not with a mouth filled with too much food.

They ate in comfortable silence, the only sounds the music in the background and the scraping of silverware on the plate they were sharing. Dean didn't remember being this content before coming back to California. He didn't need to prove anything to anyone. He didn't need to fall back on his usual personality - boisterous and charming and slightly dirty. He didn't have to worry about pining for anyone who came before Clara because they were irrelevant. Once they finished having sex, she would get her things and go and that was that. It wasn't mean - it was a mutual unspoken agreement. With Clara, he was happy. He couldn't stop himself from smiling. He had to be around her, always. He didn't want to even think about what would happen when she decided she would go - where?

Certainly not with Bill. Maybe her parents? Seraphina?

"Do you want anything else?" Dean jumped up and grabbed her plate and silverware before putting it in the sink. He needed an excuse to keep her with him. "A drink, maybe some fruit?"

Did he even have fruit?

Clara smiled. "When did you ever become such a gracious host?" she asked. "Usually, after sex, you always passed out."

Dean felt himself grin. He liked that she was comfortable enough to take shots at him. He went to the fridge and grabbed a carton of pineapple orange banana juice. Clara had been the one to introduce him to it and he was surprised to find he actually liked it - but only with ice. If there was no ice, it was too sweet.

"Do you want juice?" he asked.

"Sure."

He grabbed two glasses and filled them up with cubes of ice. "So," he said slowly. Once both glasses were both half-filled with ice, he grabbed the carton of juice and shook it up. He uncapped it and poured the juice into the glass. "What's next for you?"

He watched as Clara furrowed her brow and rolled her shoulders back. She murmured a quick, "thanks," and took the glass from him before taking a sip. Dean took his seat next to her, the ice cubes tinkling against the glass.

"What do you mean?" she asked.

"Where do you go from here?" He tapped the cool condensation on the glass. "My house is your house, Clara. That will never change. Stay as long as you want. Stay forever if you want."

Clara grinned. "You're always quick to ask me to move in with you, Dean," she said. "Last time we were together it was, what, a couple of weeks?"

"You were crazy enough to agree," he pointed out.

Clara took another sip of juice.

"I'm serious, though," he said. "Do you need me to go help you pack? Should we call your mom?"

"Dean, I honestly have no idea what I'm going to do," she admitted. She put her glass down and started rubbing her temples. "I haven't really thought about it, to be honest." She offered him a tired smile. "I know I won't be with Bill anymore. I'm sure at some point I'm going to pack up my stuff. But I don't think I want to involve you - not when you have so much on your plate already. I don't want you to worry about me."

"Clara..." He let out a breath, grasping for words he couldn't hold onto. He didn't know what he wanted he wanted to say or how to say it.

Before Dean could say anything else, Clara reached out and placed her hands on his thighs and leaned towards him. He could feel how cold her hands were through the thin material of his pajama pants, thanks to the glass of juice she had been holding.

"Dean," she murmured, "I just want to be distracted for a

bit. I want to go to a movie or eat a bunch of pie. I don't want to think about the future right this second. I just want to be with you."

Dean nodded, a small smile on his face. "I think I can help you with that," he said.

Bill would wait. But Dean wouldn't forget him. Not when he had done what he did to Clara. No one who does that gets off that easily.

# Chapter 15

THE PROBLEM with Dean was that it was too easy for Clara to fall in love with him. He was just as she remembered, only older and more experienced. They could fall back into their easy rhythm without even trying. It was like she never left. Whoever taught him about that thing he did with his tongue should be blessed on so many levels. It was easy to forget that they had had their share of problems like any other couple. It was easy to forget that she was older now too, that she was a grown woman with a job and goals and a plan for her life. It was easy to forget that they broke up for a reason, that she had been avoiding him for a reason.

Dean was a fantasy, sure, but could he be her reality again?

Looking up at the ceiling in his room, arm over her forehead, listening to him snore softly beside her, she couldn't help but ponder the question. It was ridiculous, certainly, because sex did not translate into a relationship, and just because he had rescued her a couple of times - even though she didn't need rescuing - didn't mean that they were well on their way to a new relationship. She wasn't sure if she wanted a new relationship with him, that was the problem. She needed to figure out what she wanted, and then take proper action accordingly. It was easy to love him when things were going well, but what about when they fought? And she knew his temper, knew her own; fighting was practically a guarantee. Was she ready to go back to that? And if it was so easy to slip back into their routine when things were good, would the same happen when things were bad? Would she be the Clara she was now? She didn't know if she would simply fall into her nineteen-year-old self, plagued with bad habits she had worked hard growing out of.

She didn't want that. She had worked hard to change, to be more than that nineteen year old who was self-conscious and insecure, who had a quick temper with an even faster reaction time. She was more than that; she, too, was older and more experienced. She needed to remember that.

More than that, she didn't want to fall into bad habits that she worked so hard to shed from her life, like it was some sort of second skin.

But maybe that wouldn't happen with Dean. Maybe it would be different.

Clara supposed the best thing she could do right now was figure out what she wanted. Did she want to be with Dean? What would that mean? Would he even be able to be with her, considering his reputation? Everyone had to settle down. Hell, even Zachary Ryan, Alec Schumacher, and Art Jackman had all found someone worth changing for.

Dean, on the other hand...

Did Dean even want that? Even if it was with her? Sure, they could have fun, but Clara wanted more than that. She wanted to be with him because she wanted to settle down with him. At least, she was leaning towards that. She just wished she knew what Dean wanted. She wished she could read that mind of his.

Clara rolled on her side, making sure she didn't disturb Dean behind her. She knew Dean was loyal, at least when he committed to her. Nobody said it would last between them. People said she had been crazy for moving in with him so fast.

But she did it anyway, probably because she was nineteen and stubborn and thought Dean was cute and charming.

Dean had a reputation in the NHL then, and he had one now. She just wanted to make sure he was as committed to her as she would be to him.

He had been the last time they were together. That was what people didn't understand. He could be loyal when he wanted to be, when he chose that. If someone was trying to force it, that would be a different story. Nobody could force Dean to do anything, not even her, which was why she never tried.

Now, though…

Now, she wasn't sure about anything anymore. She thought she knew what she wanted. She thought she knew she *didn't* want Dean. But everything had changed the second she saw him again.

*Everything.*

*And Bill?* a voice pointed out.

Clara blew out a breath and started playing with the ends of her hair, even though her focus was on the dark blue wall in front of her. Bill was a jerk, there was no question about that. What hurt her about Bill the most was that he actually slapped her. He could say whatever he wanted about her and that would be that, but the fact that he lost his temper and actually slapped her because she had pushed his buttons? She couldn't even fathom it. Never did she think he would ever hit her. And she wasn't going to stick around to see if and when he would do it again.

Even if he was upset about what she said to him - and honestly, it was a shitty thing for her to say, regardless of what happened between them - she didn't deserve what he did to her. He could be angry all he wanted. Hell, he could leave her over it and she would understand. But slapping her?

That crossed a line.

And what kind of woman would she be if she stayed?

He would lose all respect for her. Hell, she would too. The

relationship between them would never be the same because in the back of his mind, he would know he had slapped her and got away with it, and she would know she didn't love herself enough to respect herself. And she didn't think she could live without loving herself.

Clara had already decided she was done with Bill the minute she left, but now, she needed to get her things. For the time being, she could stay here with Dean until she found a small place of her own. Granted, she might have to move up to North County just because it was expensive living by herself with a paycheck that wasn't guaranteed - as a private investigator, she hadn't had a job for the last couple of weeks, and she felt it. She didn't want to assume anything would happen with Dean. She didn't want to assume he was serious about moving in. She wanted to be able to take care of herself. She didn't want to *need* him. If anything, she wanted to know she could rely on herself when things got hard. Which meant doing little things, like not running from her problems and getting her car.

It wasn't as though she was saying she didn't want Dean's help. She wasn't that stubborn. What she wanted, though, was knowing if nobody else was there for her, she could be. That was the most important thing to her.

She slowly peeled herself away and grabbed her phone. It had been off for her entire time with Dean and, as she pulled on a shirt and her pajama pants, she waited for her phone to turn on. She tilted her head to the side, stretching her neck, and then did the same thing to the other. When she finished, she rolled her shoulders back, stifling a yawn.

She snuck out of the room and headed down the stairs as she searched for the person she wanted to call.

Seraphina Hanson answered on the third ring.

"Hello?"

Clara bit back a smile. She was almost expecting Seraphim to be like all the other billion-dollar CEO's who answered with their name or something equally as pompous. Instead, she sounded like a regular person - but that was Seraphina for you.

"Seraphina? It's Clara."

"Clara!" Seraphina's genuine tone made Clara feel warm and fuzzy. Seraphina was the sort of friend she could count on, even if they hadn't spoken in a while. "I haven't talked to you forever! How are you?"

"Actually, I'm in a bit of a bind..."

Half an hour later, Seraphina texted her to let her know she was outside. Dean still hadn't woken up and there was no way Clara was going to wake him up to say goodbye. Dean would insist on coming with her, claiming she needed protection. More than that, Dean had a huge game tomorrow that Clara refused to distract him from. If he needed sleep - and clearly he did if he was napping so deeply - she refused to bother him with her problems. Maybe they could talk later, but right now, he needed to focus on himself and she needed to confront her problems head on. She couldn't push this back any longer. If anything, she wanted to get this over with.

Clara had her phone and headed out the door. Seraphina was driving her old Nissan. All that money, and Clara had no idea why the woman couldn't get a car that matched her bank account. Seraphina, of course, didn't seemed bugged by it one way or the other and if Seraphim didn't care, no one else should either.

"I brought you a change of clothes," Seraphina said the minute Clara slid into the passenger seat, "since we're practically the same size. Did you need anything else?"

"You are a lifesaver," Clara said, taking the clothes. She was glad it had gotten cloudy and she hoped as Seraphina slowly drove down the residential street, no one would notice as she pulled on an old Jackass t-shirt and skinny jeans. "Although... Johnny Knoxville?"

Seraphina shrugged, her lips tugging up into a grin. "What can I say?" she said. "I had a thing for bad boys."

"Had?" Clara snorted, pulling on her seatbelt. "Aren't you dating Brandon Thorpe? You know he's the quintessential NHL bad boy, except he hasn't actually been charged with a crime." She grinned. "Yet."

"My dating life is no one's concern," Seraphina said, but she was smiling. "So, not to pry, but is everything okay? I'm sure you could have had your mom come down here, or a friend. Especially since I am aware where all of my players live, and know that you just walked out of Dean Morgan's ridiculously big house. And I mean that because no one else lives there with him."

Clara looked down at her hands buried tightly between her thighs. "Honestly, Seraphina, without being weird about it, you're the closest friend I have," she admitted. "Dean and I dated the summer before my sophomore year of college. Once we broke up, I kept to myself. Obviously, I had friends at school but they were my school friends, no one I saw outside of school. And I started working after I graduated. Being a PI is a lonely profession. I only met Bill because Graham Winsor hired me for a case. Anyway, to make an already too-long story short, you were the first person I thought of, the first person I called."

Seraphina reached out and placed her hand on Clara's forearm. Clara's mouth dropped open and she looked at Seraphina.

"I'm glad," she said. "I'm here for you, Clara."

Clara felt her lips turn up as Seraphina returned her hand to the steering wheel. She looked down at her lap, pressing her palms flat on her thighs. She was so grateful for Seraphina right now, tears blurred her vision. She quickly blinked them away.

The drive was relatively silent, save for the latest Taylor Swift CD coming from the speakers. Seraphina whisper-sang the songs, moving her shoulders and bobbing her head to the beat. Clara felt her smile widen. This was normal. It felt good to be around a successful, inspirational woman who also had gone through her share of hardship and managed to come out happy and unjaded - she wasn't concerned about what Clara thought of her singing and she trusted Brandon Thorpe enough to let him in. And Seraphina had been through much more than just a slap on the face. Not to downplay what Clara had gone through, but Seraphina's journey gave Clara hope.

Thanks to Clara's directions, Seraphina got them there in ten minutes. It helped that it was a Monday morning - just after eleven o'clock - so the roads weren't filled with commuters trying to get to important lunch meetings.

"Want me to stay?" Seraphina asked, glancing up at the tall apartment complex. "I can help you move things."

"I really appreciate that," Clara said, turning to look over at Seraphina. "I have my car, and I don't plan to get tons of stuff. I just want a nice change of clothes - besides the jeans and the shirt you got me. Which I will get back to you as soon as possible. Plus, this is probably a crazy time for you right now. There's no need to waste another moment on me when you have other things you could be worrying about."

"It's not a waste," Seraphina gently corrected. "Not when we're friends." She nestled further into the cracked leather of the seat. "Call me when you're on the way to Dean's place so I know you're good."

Clara nodded. There was a slight feeling of guilt - perhaps she should tell Seraphina what happened with Bill. But if she did that, then Seraphina would stay. Seraphina would concern herself with Clara instead of focusing on her hockey team. On the fact that not only did they make the playoffs for the first time, they were battling for the Stanley Cup.

Clara headed into the building. Seraphina didn't take off until Clara was inside. The sight made Clara feel warm inside. It felt nice to be protected. It made her feel worthy.

She reached into her pocket, making sure her phone hadn't slipped out. She also found her keys. It probably would have been easier if she had just taken her car instead of riding with Dean, but after what happened, Clara didn't want to be on her own and she highly doubted Dean would let her be anyway.

The elevator ride up felt longer than it should have. Once she emerged from the steel doors, she took a step in time with her heartbeat. When she finally reached her door, she pulled out her keys. They wouldn't stop clinging together. She was nervous, she realized. She was worried Bill would be home and –

And what?

Did she really think Bill was going to do something like that again? Her face stung even though no one had touched it in hours. It was as though her face recalled what had happened and wanted to warn Clara that there was a chance of it happening again.

Clara unlocked the door and went in. In all honesty, Clara didn't know what to expect from Bill - and that was what scared her the most. She did not know if he would fly into a rage and do something worse than what he had already done, or if he would deflate, the realization of what he had done shocking him into wariness.

The apartment was still, but that didn't mean Bill wasn't there.

"Bill?" she called as she shut the door behind her. "I'm going to grab a few things."

Nothing.

Her heart still pounded but after a quick check to make sure he wasn't in the shower - he was not - Clara began to rush to get everything she wanted together so she could get out of here as fast as she could. She didn't know if Dean would still be sleeping or not, but now that she had her wallet, she would be able to pick up a couple of burgers and shakes from Wedge Burger on Seventeenth Street in hopes of alleviating any frustration he might feel over her coming here alone.

The first place she hit up was the closet. She pulled different clothes from their hangers and threw them on her bed. Jeans, slacks, yoga pants were next, followed by shoes. She stuffed everything she could into a durable black garbage bag before grabbing a second one and starting on the shoes.

Next, she emptied the bathroom and grabbed her laptop, left untouched in its case. Thank God.

When she was finished, she stepped back. There was at least two runs to her car, probably three. She glanced at the door, held her breath.

Nothing.

She grabbed the bags first and managed to stuff them into her trunk before deciding to dash up the stairs rather than the elevator. She rushed the second load too.

Almost done.

All that was left was her laptop case and her chargers.

Clara swung it across her chest and turned to go, just as the door opened and Bill walked in.

"Clara?" he asked, confused. "What are you doing?"

# Chapter 16

WHEN DEAN WOKE UP, he was alone. He shouldn't have been surprised. He knew there was a good chance that whatever was going on between him and Clara might not last - probably wouldn't - even if he wanted it to.

And he realized he wanted it to.

He immediately felt a gaping hole, a coldness where none had been before. To have her back, only to lose her for a third time was unfathomable. He needed her. Wanted her. All of that. No one else would do.

He missed her and he had just been holding her. He wanted to claim her so soon after doing just that. He didn't understand this incessant need to want it all when he had been used to living without her. He had been fine. This was ridiculous. He wasn't the sort of person to get so wound up around one person when he missed them.

But Clara was different. Dammit, she had always been different - and he knew this. He knew this.

He hoped she was just downstairs. Where else could she have gone? She didn't have her car. Granted, she could have borrowed his car and it wouldn't have been an issue. He wouldn't have cared. But it would be nice to know where she went off to, when she was planning on coming back.

Was she planning on coming back? Maybe karma finally got him. After breaking hearts left and right with no real regard for anyone save for himself, maybe karma finally decided enough was enough.

His heart skipped a beat at the thought. He didn't want her gone for good. He wanted her. Hell, he'd marry her right now if he genuinely thought she would take him.

He didn't, though.

He ran his fingers through his hair before hopping out of bed and pulling on his sweatpants. A quick glance at his phone told him it was just after three o'clock. That sounded about right. He would have a few hours to do low-intensity workouts, have a healthy dinner, maybe watch a couple of hours of television before turning in early and trying to get a good night's sleep before waking up early and getting ready for the game.

But his mind was on Clara. He was silent for a moment, but it didn't sound as though she was in the shower. He would hope that if she was going to shower, she would invite him to shower as well. There was a low intensity workout he could definitely participate in and feel good about at the same time. But that was only if she was coming back.

*Fuck, don't think like that. Don't be a fucking pussy. Jesus.*

He padded down the staircase, his head going left and right. Nothing tickled his nose. Not that Clara gave him the impression that she would ever cook - because he knew from personal experience that she was not the sort of woman to cook - but he didn't know if that had changed in the nine years they hadn't seen each other.

He tried to ignore the disappointed skip of his heart, tried to ignore the knot of disappointment sinking in his stomach.

Dean walked into the kitchen.

Empty.

But there was a piece of paper on the fridge. It hadn't been there before.

He held his breath and walked over to it.

He moved the magnet to the side and he pulled the paper from where it rested. *Be right back. C.*

That explained nothing.

But at least it meant that she was coming back.

His lips twitched. He swallowed, trying to push down the gurgle of happiness.

She was coming back.

Dean decided the best thing he could do at this point was call her but he was sent to voicemail. His heart skipped a beat and he roused from his post-nap haze. If his call was being sent to voicemail that could mean one of two things: it died and she completely forgot to charge it, which was plausible; or she was purposefully sending it there.

Why would she do that?

He crossed his arms over his chest, heading back up the stairs. He planned to put on more clothes and brush his teeth. Maybe he should actually shower and take some time to ready himself for when she came back.

She would come back. The note said as much.

But there was something that began to prickle at the base of his neck, something that left him much more unsettled than he cared to admit. He wasn't sure what it was, exactly, other than a feeling.

Not an emotion, but something in his gut that just ate at him, telling him something.

The problem was, he wasn't sure what the feeling was saying in the first place.

Did it have to do with the note? Were her words merely words - lies she scrawled on paper just to appease him, to ensure he didn't come after her?

He shouldn't care - but he did. He wanted her to come back. Maybe it was sudden, his asking her to move in, and the last thing he wanted to make her feel was discomfort. But he did want her to know that she was always welcome at his place, even if she needed time to get back on her feet.

Dean shook his head. Let him shower. Maybe by that point she'd be back. They could talk. The feeling would settle down.

He was just letting this get into his head. He was starting to doubt himself. Now that he finally had her, now that he had everything he could possibly want, he worried it would slip away as easily as it had come to him in the first place.

The problem was, Dean took quick showers. Ten minutes tops - and then he was done. Ready to get out. He had never been one for bathing, for washing, even as a kid. Now, he didn't mind it because there was a reason for it, but he still didn't stick around for a while if he could help it.

After stepping out and drying off, he got dressed, brushed his teeth, and slicked his hair back using only the water. He checked his phone but saw no change. No call from Clara. No text. A quick call to her phone and it went right to voicemail again.

How the hell did she leave? That was what Dean wanted to know. She didn't have a car. He drove her here. Had she taken one of his?

His feet led him to his garage but found all three vehicles still parked. He continued to frown, his hands on his hips. Now what?

The feeling that had simmered in the shower began to claw at his insides once more.

Suddenly, his phone chimed. He practically ripped it out of his pocket and brought it up to read the text, but found it was only from Seraphina Hanson rather than Clara. He couldn't help but feel slightly disappointed and then found himself feeling guilty for being disappointed. Seraphina was one hell of a GM and he was lucky to have her as a boss.

*How's Clara? I tried calling but it's going straight to voicemail.*

Dean frowned. He began to pace up and down his living

room, his thumb hovering on the call button. Why would Seraphina ask about Clara - unless Clara called her. Unless Seraphina was Clara's ride to... where? Well, if Dean wanted to think in his favor - and he always did - maybe Clara called Seraphina for a ride to get her stuff and come back to Dean's. But if Seraphina was Clara's ride, why did Seraphina leave her?

Unless...

Unless...

Dean felt his thoughts churning and spinning. He shoved his phone in his pocket and grabbed his keys. Clara was at her old place. She planned to come back to Dean's place judging from the note still on his refrigerator. Clara could have called Seraphina to take her over to her old place. Her car was there and there was no way Clara would have Seraphina stick around while she grabbed all of the things she wanted to take with her - at least, Dean assumed. If she was as stubborn now as she was then, he wouldn't be surprised if Clara told her to leave. Dean knew Seraphina; Seraphina would have asked if she needed help. No, Clara sent Seraphina away.

Dean decided to drive the SUV. In case Clara needed help with her stuff, he wanted to be there to help her out. He didn't want anything being left behind. He wanted her safe from Bill - completely this time.

He started the engine and clicked his garage door button. While he waited for the garage door to ascend, he shot Seraphina a quick message, telling her he was going to check on Clara now and that he'd call her later today with an update. From there, he pulled out of his driveway, closed his garage door, and was off.

His tapped his thumb against the wheel as he tried to drive as fast as he could without getting caught. It was a tricky thing since he wasn't a fan of weaving in and out of cars, but he didn't know how Bill would react to seeing Clara there - if Bill would even be there in the first place - and he wanted to ensure that Clara was safe.

*Why couldn't she have said anything?*

He tried not to let himself get caught up in the fact that Clara didn't wake him up specifically to tell him where she was going. Granted, he knew she probably knew he wouldn't react well. Maybe she figured she wanted to handle this on her own, like an independent woman.

He could respect that. He could.

But he wanted to be there to help. If she wanted him to be.

Dean squeezed the wheel tightly, trying not to grind his teeth. He knew without a doubt that Clara had no intention of going back to Bill. She had always respected herself too much to be with someone who would treat her like shit. He knew that. Even when they were together and his fiery temper caused a rift between them, she would stand up for herself. At the time, her stubbornness would grate on his nerves, but if they ever had a daughter -

No, too soon.

Too soon to think about starting a family.

They hadn't even discussed being together again. Having sex a few times did not mean they were together. It meant...

He didn't know what it meant. He would figure that out later. What he needed to focus on was Clara.

When he pulled up to her old place, Dean hesitated. Did she even need his help? He didn't want to stroll in and make her feel incapable. Another part of him wanted to make sure she knew he was there for her, that she could count on him, that she could trust him to always have her back because he didn't have it before and he regretted that now. He regretted that more than anything.

In the end, his journey had brought him back to her. They were together again - at least physically.

Dean parked his car next to the leasing office. If his car got towed, fuck it. He didn't care. Using his memory, he headed inside and pressed the elevator button. A teenage boy ran up to him, excited about the fact that the Gulls were in the finals for the first time in their tenure and asked for a quick selfie. Dean obliged just as the elevator doors slid open. After thanking the kid, Dean stepped inside and rubbed his hands together, heaving a sigh.

He was nervous, but didn't understand why he was nervous.

The elevator pinged when he reached her floor. He stepped out, pausing just to take another breath.

What if she didn't need him? What if she didn't want him? What if -

He shook his head.

*Get your shit together, man,* he snapped at himself.

He strode down the long hallway, his arms moving by his sides. He had no idea what to do with his hands. At first, he shoved them in his pockets but found that that didn't work. Next, he tried his back pockets, then his hips, until he finally dropped his hands and let them fall altogether.

He saw her door. It was closed but he could hear voices coming from inside. He shouldn't listen. It wasn't his place. It wasn't his business. But he needed to make sure she wasn't upset.

"...fucking Dean Morgan!"

"What I do now is none of your business, Bill." Clara's snappy response didn't surprise him in the least. She always got flippant when she was pissed off. She didn't have to use her hands in order hurt someone. "We're through."

A pause. Dean couldn't be sure but it almost sounded like one of them sighed. Quite possibly Bill. If it was one of frustration or one of relent, Dean couldn't be sure.

"Look, Clara, I'm —"

"Please don't tell me you're apologizing." Clara's voice was flat. Dean recognized that voice. Clara had checked out. She was done. Dean himself had heard that voice on multiple occasions.

"I'm not trying to justify what I did." A pause. A quiver in his voice. Dean felt something inside of him coil. He didn't want to admit it but it almost sounded as though Bill was actually sincere. "What I did was... deplorable. Inexcusable. Disgusting. I'm not saying I deserve a second chance. I'm not even asking for one. I just... I just want you to know that you don't deserve that. I completely understand why you're leaving, okay?"

"If you knew that, why fight? Why even bring Dean up? He has nothing to do with this."

"He has everything to do with this!" Bill exclaimed.

Dean reached for the door, ready to break it down if he needed to. No one was allowed to talk to her that way.

"Don't talk to me that way," Clara snapped. Dean felt his lips quirk up. He dropped his hand and bit back a smirk. He shouldn't have assumed Clara needed his help. She was handling this herself nicely. "Dean has nothing to do with this. I should have told you about him before. I take responsibility for that. But you? You should have believed me. You should have stayed with me in the parking lot. You shouldn't have left me the way you did. But you did. And you should have told me you weren't coming home. To this second, I haven't pushed about where you went that night. I trust you. I've always trusted you. But clearly, you couldn't give me that same respect."

There was a pause. Dean expected Clara took a breath, something like that.

"I don't need you to tell me how deplorable your behavior was, Bill. I know it. It's why I'm so incredibly furious with you. I just - I just never expected this from you. I thought you were different, but you aren't."

"You're fucking him, aren't you?"

"That's none of your business, Bill."

"Just tell me. Just tell me, just be honest, and then we can go our separate ways. I just… I just want to know. I need to know."

"I don't have to - hey, let go of my arm! I'm not going to tell you anything."

Dean didn't wait any longer. Clara could certainly handle herself, but Bill couldn't respect her enough not to touch her.

Fuck him. Fuck being nice.

Dean was not about to let this asshole put his hands on Dean's girl again.

With that, he threw open the door, his knuckles itching for something to hit.

# Chapter 17

CLARA'S HEART lodged itself in her throat the minute Bill grabbed her arm. He had just asked her a question and she froze. She hadn't been expecting him at all, and now that he was here, now that he was in front of her, she had no idea what to do. Maybe he wasn't planning on doing anything. Maybe this wasn't something where she would need to worry about him hurting her again. But the fact that he lunged for her, the fact that he had to grab onto her even though he probably should be sensitive to stuff like that, didn't bode well. She wasn't sure it actually meant anything but it didn't actually matter. She could see the look in his eyes - the flash of anger, like lightning. Why he was angry, she wasn't sure, until she remembered what she was doing, what she must look like.

She was packing up her things. She was sneaking away without saying anything to him at all.

Clara had no intention of sticking around to see if lightning struck twice. She yanked her arm from Bill and managed to pull it away from his grasp. However, her force was so much that she stumbled backwards a couple of times, only to run into the chest of someone.

Someone familiar.

Clara glanced up and saw Dean's chiseled face contorted into a scowl as he looked at Bill. How he had gotten here, how he even knew where she was, Clara had no idea. But the sense of relief that filled her body the second she laid eyes on him was enough to calm her down, if only slightly. His nostrils were flared like an animal, his eyes slicing through the space between him and Bill like a knife. There was anger there as well, just like with Bill. Clara could feel it. But unlike Bill, she trusted Dean. Still, she knew him, knew what he was capable of. While she appreciated his protectiveness, Bill wasn't worth it, wasn't worth injuring himself over or causing enough harm to the point where Bill felt compelled to press charges. She took in a deep breath and decided this needed to de-escalate as quickly as possible, and she was the only person who could do that.

"What did I tell you about touching my girl again?" Dean took a step forward, causing Clara to straighten. It was as though she wasn't even there. Dean's focus was only on Bill, and Clara nearly stumbled again.

She was supposed to be calming the two of them down. The problem was, Clara got distracted. His girl? When had they talked about the nature of their relationship? Granted, Clara wanted to be with Dean. There wasn't a doubt about that, especially after she had taken time away from Dean to truly figure that out. In what capacity, Clara couldn't say as of yet. But she knew she was over Bill. She knew she still had feelings for Dean. She knew she wanted to explore those feelings. And she knew that Dean could injure himself or get into a lot of trouble if she didn't get him out of here now.

"Your girl?" Bill's eyes shifted over to Clara. His eyes had tempered the anger. If anything, he almost looked as though he might have apologized, that maybe, just maybe, they would go their separate ways without animosity between them, went out the window. Now, the anger was back, and it was worse than lightning, worse than anything else, because it wasn't just her he was upset with, but Dean as well. And there was a good chance he might take it out on her. "What do you mean, your girl? Just because you were with her before doesn't mean she's yours. You know this, right?"

"Sure it does," Dean said. Clara could see the flicker of the corner of his lips, the sparkle in his eye. However, she knew he wasn't amused. There was no reason to be amused. And Bill was sensitive to being laughed at. It was something she hadn't really thought about, not until she saw it in works with Dean, but Bill cared very deeply about being taken seriously. If someone like Dean strolled in and began to laugh at his thoughts, it wasn't going to go over well. "She's always been mine. You just didn't know it. Or, from what Clara told me, you just didn't believe it."

Clara wanted to roll her eyes. She knew Dean didn't actually believe that. She knew Dean didn't think she was an object that belonged to him just because they dated previously and he had come before Bill. Clara knew he was saying this just to piss off Bill, which was stupid because it was clear Bill was already pissed off. Dean didn't need to make it worse. Even so, that didn't mean she had to like that he was saying this in the first place. She was going to have a talk with him about this afterwards, that was for sure.

She just needed there to be an afterward. She needed for her and Dean to be okay. Hell, she even wanted Bill to be okay. But first, she wanted him away from her, out of her life, so she didn't have to deal with this...tension.

"Is that right?" Bill didn't believe him either. Clara hated to admit it, but Bill knew her better than a lot of people. They had been together seriously for just under a year. He knew she didn't appreciate being anyone's possession. "Then why has she been crawling into my bed every night the past ten months? Why has she been spreading her legs for me every night? Why is it my name on her lips when I get her to twitch around —"

"That's enough." Clara couldn't help but cut him off. She glared at both of them, her face an ugly shade of red due to Bill's unnecessary graphic description.

"Clearly she wasn't satisfied with your cookie cutter performance," Dean said with a nonchalant shrug. "Why else would she come back to me?"

Clara felt like she had been punched in the gut. Now Dean was playing this stupid game as well? She wasn't about to stick around to see what either of them said next.

Without another word, she stepped around Dean and headed straight for the stairway. Her eyes were blurred with tears but she refused to wipe them away. Doing so would acknowledge them and she was not in the right frame of mind where she wanted to acknowledge them. She pushed the door open and headed down the stairs, hurrying as she did so. One tear fell, and then another. They were slow-moving, not terribly noticeable.

She managed to get to her car without anything - or anyone - prohibiting her from doing so. In that way, it was almost worse. Not that she expected Dean to run after her like they were in a Hallmark movie, but it would have been nice for him to recognize that she didn't want to watch them play who had the biggest dick. She started her car and was just about to shift gears into reverse, when someone knocked on her window.

Clara glanced out.

Dean.

She almost drove off.

Almost.

Instead, she rolled down her window, shooting him a look that involved one raised eyebrow and a tight-lipped frown.

"You okay?" His deep voice managed to cause the hair on her neck to stand up.

Clara took a deep but shaky breath. She considered throwing him a caustic comment in hopes that he could see just how much his tactlessness hurt her. "As okay as I will ever be," she said with a shrug. Her tone was clipped and she did not bother to change that.

"Why'd you run off?" Dean asked.

Clara snorted. "Stop playing these games, Dean," she said. "I'm not in the mood."

"I have no idea what you're talking about," Dean said. Judging from the pinched brow and the tilted head, Clara could tell he was being serious.

She let out another breath, flexing her fingers on the steering wheel and shaking her head.

"What's going on?" Dean asked. "Why didn't you tell me that you were coming here?"

"You actually think I would come back to this asshole?" Clara demanded. Her body was pinched with energy. She could feel it thrumming through her, needing some sort of outlet. Some sort of release. "You actually think I would –"

"Of course not," Dean snapped, though he kept his voice low. "You respect yourself too much to put up with shit like that. You didn't put up with half the shit I did and I never did anything like that to you."

Clara felt herself calm down, hearing him speak. It was nice to know he saw her the way she did herself. Still, she had to tighten her grip on the steering wheel, her fingers shaking.

"No," she agreed. "You never did anything like that."

"So, what is it?" Dean crossed his arms over his chest and gave her a look.

"I just –"

"Don't trust me."

Clara picked her eyes off the concrete so she could meet his. Hard blue eyes. He was protecting himself, preparing for the worst. She wasn't sure if she should be understanding or offended. Maybe the fact that she couldn't even figure out how to react was enough of an answer.

The past two days had been a whirlwind. So much had happened and Clara hadn't had the time to breathe, to let everything sink in, to really think what this meant to her.

"You're wrong."

Clara glanced to her car and shifted her weight. She saw all of her things, things that belonged solely to her, somehow fit into her small car. She could get into the driver's seat and leave. She could go anywhere she wanted, start over. The thought was depressing. She didn't want to run away. She wanted to grow roots. She wanted to belong. She wanted to get more clients, bring in steady income. She wanted to stand on her own two feet.

"I trust you more than you think I do." Her voice got stronger with each word. "I trust you more than even I realize."

"Then why –"

"I think," Clara said. She knew she was interrupting him and she knew he was doing a great job, much better than he had before, with his patience for that. She pressed her lips together, a small smile on her face. "Sorry. I don't mean to interrupt." She looked up at him, hoping to reflect nothing but honesty in return. "I think I needed to do this on my own. I really appreciate all you've done so far. I have. But I needed to do this on my own. I really feel like I need to be the one to handle this. And you being there... it might not help things. Not in a bad way, but –"

"It'll make it harder for you," Dean said.

Clara nodded. "Exactly," she said. "And, like I said, I love having you with me, I love knowing that you're here with me no matter what, but at the same time, I need to do what's best for me first. I feel after you left the first time, I was gutted. Seriously, gutted. It took me months before I was able to pick myself back up. And this isn't anything against you. You did what you had to do for you and what was best for you. I don't blame you."

"Clara." His voice was short but not rude. More like she was babbling and he wanted to calm her down so he could speak. "Clara."

She stopped talking. Clara felt her cheeks turn pink under the penetrating gaze of his blue eyes. They scanned her face, the contours of her cheeks. She looked away, shifting her weight.

She wasn't comfortable feeling so... noticed before, even if she was noticed by him.

"Yes?" she asked. "I'm sorry, am I talking too much?"

"You always talk too much," he said. The corners of his lips flicked up in amusement. "But actually, I just wanted to let you know that I'm here to support you."

Clara blinked. She shouldn't have been surprised, but she was. Not that Dean was supportive, but that he was willing to let her do this her way, without offering an opinion of how to do it better.

"If you support me, why compete with Bill?" she pushed. She placed one hand on her hips and narrowed her eyes. "Bill said some pretty messed up stuff about me. But you didn't help the situation by egging him on."

"What are you —" Dean cut himself off and looked away. "Oh." He shook his head. "I wasn't trying to say that we fucked or anything like that. I was trying to tell him that regardless of all the great things he thinks he has over you, you still chose... I'm not going to win you over on this, am I?"

Clara smirked, shaking her head. "See, that? That right there doesn't help me."

"I know you're right, but I wanted to knock the asshole down. I couldn't use my fists. He didn't give me a reason to, though I probably would have just for grabbing your arm in that way."

Clara sighed and glanced away. She heard seagulls cawing. The beach was a five minute drive from these apartments. She would miss being so close to the ocean. Some nights, if it was especially quiet, she could hear the waves crashing on the shore and she would think how perfect life was in that moment.

"I'm glad you decided not to indulge," Clara said, her voice flat. "It doesn't help me when you integrate yourself into my issues with Bill. His whole thing is that I left because of you and not because of what he did. Obviously we know that isn't true, but he needs to know that. And when you say dumb stuff like that, whether you mean it or not, you give him an excuse he wouldn't have had otherwise."

Dean took a step back. Clara wasn't sure why he felt he needed to put space between them but she wasn't going to judge him. Her goal was telling him the truth and she felt as though she was doing as good of a job as she could hope for.

"We need to talk," he said finally, pulling his eyes away from scanning the rows of cars parked in the structure, even during the day. "But now isn't the appropriate time to do that."

Clara felt herself move closer to her car at his words. She knew he was right. She knew this. And yet, her shoulders felt stiff and heavy, like she was suddenly carrying a weight she couldn't quite shoulder.

"When do you want to do that?" Clara forced herself to ask, her voice dry.

"Tonight." He glanced back at the structure. "Once you're ready. If that's okay with you."

Clara nodded once. "Sounds like a plan," she agreed.

"Where are you off to now?" Dean asked, nodding at the car.

"I'll probably take this to your place," Clara admitted, "and then I'll take some time to myself. Just to get clarity."

## Chapter 18

CLARITY WAS NOT something Clara actively sought out before. She didn't know she needed to, up until she was at a crossroads and a decision about her life had to be made.

At the end of the day, she just needed to figure out what she wanted. That was it. As simple as that sounded, it wasn't so easy to come by. There were voices in her head, reminding her of Dean's imperfections, how he used to act, how he would never commit to her. There were voices telling her never to go back to sloppy seconds, that people never really changed. There were voices saying he wasn't right for her.

But, when it all came out, she realized she wanted to be with Dean. It didn't have to make sense. It didn't have to look good on paper. It was just a feeling she needed to unravel, something she needed to claim for herself. And when it came to Dean, she was ready to put her heart on the line and claim him, no matter the risk.

▭

CLARA HADN'T GOTTEN home until late that night and she crawled in Dean's bed with no indication that she wanted to fool around. Dean could appreciate the gesture. Granted, he didn't know if she was doing this out of respect or if she didn't want to jump back in the sack with him. There was part of him that knew Clara well enough to know that even with their history, she wasn't in any kind of rush to rekindle that flame that had set them on fire so long ago. He knew it wouldn't get to that point this quickly. He also knew he needed his own adjustment period to this relationship - or whatever this was. As much as he knew he wanted Clara to be with him, he needed some time to sort all of it out. Not because he had any doubts, but because their relationship deserved that level of respect and consideration - two things he hadn't really made an effort to give it back when they were first together.

What he did know was that he had a very important game today, which meant he was out of bed by six thirty in the morning. As much as he wanted o stay wrapped up in her warmth, as much as he didn't want to leave Clara so soon after he got her, he knew he had to. This game was the most important game in his entire career, and while Clara, too, was important to him, he couldn't put it aside because she suddenly showed back up in his life. Luckily for him, he knew she would understand that.

He grabbed a piece of toast, and downed a cup of black coffee. He slipped into his Jaguar, one of his superstitions, and headed to the rink for their morning skate.

For the time being, Dean put Clara out of his mind. For now, he needed to focus on the game. He needed to focus on getting that second win. He would think about Clara when he could give her the time and attention she deserved. As it was, the team needed him more than she did right now.

As he skated on the ice, he made sure to really stretch the muscles in his groin, his pelvis, his legs. He wanted to make sure they were awake and ready to move for tonight. The last thing he needed was a pulled muscle during a pivotal moment of the game. Sure, he knew he wasn't a Kyle Underwood or a Zachary

Ryan, but he liked to think that his presence on the ice did make some kind of difference, however small.

Cherney was even more of a dick than he typically was, which Dean expected. Dean wasn't sure if it was because everyone was being an asshole, but he knew tensions were high, considering there were potentially three games left - at the least - and then, the Cup was theirs. It had finally hit the majority of the team that this was it. This was what they had been playing all season for. And not just then, but every single season before that, every single in-house and club hockey game, every single five thirty AM skating practice, every single travel game, every single cardio and weight workout. This was the reason Dean had given up beer. This was the reason why he left Southern California nine years ago only to come back here, playing his former team. This was the reason he left Clara - and now there was a chance he could have her back, he could have both. He could have it *all*.

Tensions were high. Dean could feel it. Everyone could feel it.

Cherney worked them hard. Dean has never felt strain in his thighs the way he did after he got off the ice.

When they were dismissed, Brandon Thorpe cleared his throat. Instantly, the side chatter quieted and everyone gave him their full focus.

"As you know," he said, his voice soft and low, "we've had a turbulent season. But we're here. Our perseverance, our hard work, all paid off. This is our moment. It's our birthright. This is ours for the taking. Can you feel it? Can you feel the Cup in your hands as you lift it over your head? Can you hear the roar of the crowd as they're cheering 'Go Gulls'? As they're cheering your name? You should. Can you see your name etched in the cup, along with the greats? Along with Wayne Gretzky? Mario Lemieux? Bobby Orr? Sydney Crosby? Teemu Selanne? You should. It's yours. Your name is there. Every single one of our names is there. Do you believe it? Do you believe it's ours? If not, I don't want to see you back here this afternoon."

And that was it.

Dean grinned. That was probably the best damn speech he had ever heard but the best part was his ending. Thorpe knew how to end a speech.

Nothing more was said by the captain. Instead, he simply turned and skated off. Dean almost laughed. Jackman chuckled under his breath as he came over to Dean.

"Thorpe's a piece, isn't he?" Jackman asked.

Dean didn't answer. Instead, he shook his head, skating off the ice with his friend. He took a quick shower and headed back to his place. He was ready to crawl into bed and take a nap. Now that he wasn't on the ice, Clara came back to him with such force that he felt as though he was slapped across the face. By the time he pulled into his garage, his heart thudded against his chest like a kick drum. He didn't know why he was nervous, but he was.

This was Clara. *Clara*.

And yet, he could not help but feel slightly off. Unsure.

He didn't know what was going to happen. He knew what he wanted to happen but he didn't know if what he wanted and what she wanted would align. And that made him nervous.

Clara looked up at him when he walked into the kitchen. Her tousled hair framed her face, though the majority of it was pulled up into a messy bun. She was in her pajamas - comfy pants and a large t-shirt.

She looked perfect here. Like she fit.

He could get used to this.

She smiled. Her eyes lit up like fire and he couldn't help but stare.

"I see you already showered," she said, glancing down at whatever it was she was cooking.

It was only then that he noticed she was cooking something. His nostrils flared.

"I see you haven't burned the house down," he drawled. Suddenly, all thoughts of napping went out the window. He could stay and stare at her all day if she would let him. At least until the game tonight.

"Give me time," she said with a knowing grin.

"No Destiny's Child?" He glanced over at the speakers he set on top of the refrigerator. "No old school Britney Spears?"

"Not yet."

"You don't know how to work the system," Dean stated, his tone flat.

She grabbed a spatula and started flipping the pancakes. "I don't know how to work the system," she agreed.

"Watch and learn." He cleared his throat. "Alexa, play Britney Spears."

"Playing Britney Spears."

Suddenly, "Baby... One More Time" was playing from the speakers. Probably without realizing what she was doing, Clara started to move her hips side to side, bobbing her head up and down. His heart swelled at the sight. He had seen her naked, he had seen her dressed up, he had seen her in a bikini, in jeans and a shirt. For some reason, he had never seen her look so beautiful as she did in that moment.

"I love you."

The words took both of them by surprise but he refused to take it back. In fact, he felt lighter now that he had finally said them.

She blinked. It was obvious she was taken aback by his words because of her wide eyes, the way the amusement immediately disappeared from the irises.

He wasn't sorry. How could he be sorry for being honest?

Whatever happened now, however she reacted, he would deal with it. He would throw himself into the game tonight. He would push and shove and possibly take a chainsaw to his bed rather than his sofa, but he would constructively attempt to channel his frustration into something physical in order to feel better. But that was only if something bad came from this.

There was a chance that something good could come from this. There was a chance she wanted him just as much as he wanted her.

"I – I –"She flattened her hands and wiped her stomach with her palms, as though she had gotten some cooking residue on her clothes. Clara was nervous. That was obvious. "Dean, I don't know what to say."

Loss of breath. A sucker punch to the gut. But he wouldn't show it.

He forced a smile. "Just be honest, Clara," he said. "You don't even have to respond. I just..." He reached up to cup the back of his neck with his hand. He wasn't surprised to feel slight perspiration. "I just needed to say it. I needed you to know it."

Clara swallowed. His eyes homed in on the way her throat bobbed up and down. He was transfixed by it. That, or he was distracting himself from her uncharacteristic silence.

Without warning, she crossed the kitchen and launched herself into his arms so hers wrapped around his broad shoulders at the same time her legs wrapped around his waist. He caught her, but just barely, and gripped her upper thighs to keep her in his arms.

"I take it that you reciprocate the feeling?" he asked.

Clara laughed and nodded. "Sorry," she said. "That probably should have been the first thing I did. I love you, Dean. I love you. I've loved you since you left. I just... I never stopped loving you. This whole thing with Bill..." She raked her fingers through her hair while keeping her left hand firmly on his shoulder to keep her balance. "I'm glad. About everything. I'm glad it happened the way it happened."

"Clara..." He didn't agree. Regardless of the fact that he had her again with him, that she had reciprocated the emotion, that he knew she loved him, did not mean he liked what she had to endure to get them here.

"No, I'm being honest, Dean." She looked eyes with him. "You told me to be honest and that's what I'm doing. I just want you to know that. I want you to know that everything that happened, happened so you and me could be together again. It made me appreciate you. It made me realize I still loved you after all this time. And it made me realize I want to be with you. So here I am, with you." Clara's nose twitched. "What's that smell?"

Dean sniffed the air and found himself grinning. "I knew it was only a matter of time," he said. "You better turn off the stove now or you're going to burn down my house!"

DEAN TOOK IN A DEEP BREATH. He bent forward at the knees, his hockey stick horizontal as he skated slowly during the scheduled commercial break. His muscles were tight. He needed to relax them so he could move more freely.

It was the first period of the game. There was four minutes and thirty-two seconds left. Florida was already up by two. In the first fucking period.

From his position on the ice, he could see Cherney frantically scribbling something on his whiteboard in front of the players on the bench, which included Zachary Ryan, Alec Schumacher, and Kyle Underwood. There was a tension that permeated the arena. He could feel it in his bones.

Things needed to turn around.

The referee blew his whistle. The linesman skated over for a puck drop to Brandon Thorpe's left because Liam Worthington - fourth line right winger - iced the puck, which meant Dean, along with everyone else on the Gulls who had been out on the ice during the play - were forced to remain on the ice, even though they wanted nothing more than to get off the ice and catch their breath.

They were lucky they even had that commercial break. It

gave them a couple of minutes to rest before going out and starting all over again.

The four minutes went by in a flash. The Gulls didn't score, but at least Florida didn't score again.

There was a good chance Dean was going to get into a fight with Florida's enforcer, some prick named Naught who looked like Jason Statham on steroids. The guy - probably his age - was running his mouth, trying to get under his skin. Dean hated the fact that it was actually working.

The minute the buzzer sounded, he gulped down his water. The media would either interview Thorpe or one of the defensemen - probably Jackman, which meant, he was free to quiet his mind and visualize what he needed to happen so he could up his game.

On his way into the locker room, Dean looked up and caught eyes with Clara. She wasn't seated with the other wives and girlfriends. Neither of them were ready just yet to come out. It was Clara's idea. Win the Cup first, then they can figure out all the messy details of their relationship. But not until then.

"Just know," she had said as he slung his bag over his shoulder, getting ready to get to the ice, "I'll wait. You have me. Don't worry about anything else except doing everything it takes to win."

And then she kissed him like she fucking meant it, slapped his ass on the way out, and closed the door leading into the garage.

That woman was going to be the death of him.

He smirked to himself, shaking his head. Dean wouldn't have it any other way.

**The End**

Want the next book in the Slapshot Series? Book 8 is available here! Grab it now!

**Wedding Rings & Champions**

*Chapter 1*

"Get the motherfucker!"

Chris Worthington smiled at the enthusiastic Gulls fans as they pounded on the glass so hard it wobbled. Typically, he couldn't hear what was shouted at him during the games—whether from fans or coaches—but this was a special occasion. Game 7 of the Stanley Cup Finals was in Orlando, Florida, and Newport Beach Gulls fans had made the twenty-five hundred mile trek from the Southern California beach town to the home of Disney World. There were more Gulls fans here than he expected, probably because this was the first time in the twenty years of Gulls' history that the NHL team had made playoffs, much less the Stanley Cup Finals. Also because if the Gulls won this game, they were crowned as Stanley Cup Champions.

Chris didn't want to get ahead of himself. He had done that before and it always backfired. This time, he didn't want to start celebrating before there was a good reason to. He didn't want to stick his foot in his mouth, which was the worst sort of punishment.

He cracked his knuckles on each hand before slipping on his

gloves. It was a habit he developed when he was a mite, back when he was playing travel hockey through a local rink at four years old, and it had stuck with him ever since. Some called it a superstition, but he wasn't sure if he would go that far. It was a gesture that grounded him to the moment, a gesture that helped him focus on what he wanted to accomplish.

It didn't always work, but it reminded him to try, and that reminder tended to calm him down.

The fans were on their feet, screaming and shouting. They talked to Chris like they knew him, and, in a way, they did. They were the reason he had a job. They were the reason he was able to do what he did - play hockey on a professional level. He loved interacting with them off the ice - especially since they were always willing to buy him a beer.

Now, though, it was different. He didn't understand it, but there was this pressure to produce. It wasn't just about him anymore. It wasn't just about the team. It was about everyone involved. They were all part of this. The team couldn't have gotten here without the support of the fans, and they wouldn't be here without the team. They all needed each other. They all worked together to make this happen.

But Chris was on the ice. The players were on the ice.

They needed to make it happen.

Had to.

Defeat was not an option.

It was the start of the second period and Chris sat on the bench, waiting for Cherney to throw him into the game. As a third line left winger, he typically played anywhere from eleven to fifteen minutes in a sixty-minute game. It wasn't a lot, but it didn't matter. Every time his skates touched the ice, he made the most of it. He had to. He might not play for a while after he was pulled out. Making an impact, a difference, was the most impor-tant thing to him, and he made sure to do all he could in the short thirty to forty-five seconds he had in his shift.

James Negan won the faceoff and the game began.

The game was gritty, as it usually was. There seemed to be an extra amount of choppiness, only because of the inherent rivalry. It was strange to Chris - Newport Beach in California and Orlando in Floria were an entire country apart. They were part of different divisions on top of everything else. They shouldn't be rivals. He didn't know if it was because Dean Morgan came from Florida or if it was because the teams them-selves had a similar style of play - hard and fast, utilizing enforcers more than not - but there was an electrifying buzz that ran throughout the stadium. Chris felt it in his bones. It revital-ized him, made him want to play harder than ever.

It was four minutes and thirty-two seconds when Chris was finally thrown into the game. He practically leapt like some sort of ballet dancer onto the rink, landing on his blade.

Fuck, it felt like flying.

Orlando's ice was notorious for being okay at best, and he had to make sure he kept his eye out for places with too much water and a bouncing puck. Even though the Zamboni had already cleaned the ice recently, it didn't matter. The ice got bad fast, and coming from a home rink that was in the best condi-tion with the Ice Palace, it was difficult to get used to. It gave the Florida Gators an advantage, however; they knew how to play in the circumstances while Chris and the Gulls did not.

Chris kept his head down and skated after the puck. He couldn't worry about shitty ice conditions now, not when he had a game to play, a game to *win*. He crashed into a body in the boards. The impact was like adrenaline to Chris. He barely felt it. His whole body was numb to the tension, the anticipation - *everything*. Pain didn't even register.

A whistle pierced the stadium - the only thing that did finally get to Chris. He blinked once, and watched as the play stopped dead and a penalty was called.

"Bull-fucking-shit!" Chris yelled, rolling his eyes before curling his gloved fingers tight around his stick. He shouldn't be surprised - it was the clear the referees had an agenda the entire series. It was almost like the League didn't want a SoCal team to win the Cup, though Chris didn't understand why that was. Regardless of his feelings, he couldn't lose his temper. If he wasn't careful, he could get a misconduct and then thrown out of the game. And that was the last thing he wanted. He wanted to help, not make things worse. And even if the penalty was bull-fucking-shit, there wasn't anything he could do about it.

He skated over to the box—a place where skaters had to sit for a certain amount of time—while his team played short, trying to defend the opponent and their advantage. Momentum could shift with power plays. If a defending team killed it off, they might earn it. If the offenders scored, they would get it. Every move was calculated, almost desperate, and Chris wasn't part of it. When he plopped down, he let his stick fall forward, but kept hold of the shaft. He did not like to leave his stick unattended and didn't want anyone to assume he was throwing a tantrum.

Chris kept his eyes on the game. He never got nervous except when he was in the box. If they scored, even if it was a dumb penalty for the ref to have called, he always felt responsible. As such, he rarely if ever grabbed a gulp of the Gatorade placed inside the box for players, he ignored the fans that pounded on the box, trying to gather his attention. Instead, he kept his eyes peeled in front of him, focused on the game. Each time the Gulls managed to ice the puck, he felt the tension ease slightly. Each time the Gators managed to bring it back into the zone, he tensed back up.

When there were ten seconds left in his penalty, he stood. A man in a suit stood next to the door, his hand on the knob so he could whip it open for Chris the minute the countdown hit zero.

It was the longest ten seconds of the game. He glanced over at Cherney, who gestured at the net.

Good.

Chris was allowed to redeem himself and go help collect the puck in hopes to attack the Gators' zone. While he didn't agree he boarded Williams, Chris would have to make sure his hits were more agreeable. Penalties were not something he liked taking.

He took off the minute his skates touched the ice. He battled low, throwing his body where it needed to be. He managed to grab the puck and pass it up to Zachary Ryan. Ryan flew down the ice. He wasn't known for his speed. The bastard was tall and solid and had a shot Chris didn't want to stand in front of, but somehow, his feet were light, and his stickhandling was both quick and deceiving.

One slapshot and it was buried in the corner of the net.

The barn of spectators started booing but Chris could make out some of the Gulls fans standing up in their navy blue jerseys, jumping up and down, not caring that they were few.

Chris allowed himself to quirk his lips into a smile. They were on the board. One to zero. But now, they needed to focus and get another one. And then another, until the final horn sounded and the Gulls were announced as the winners.

There were no more goals scored in the game. It was Zachary Ryan's, given to him by Chris Worthington, that won the game.

Sticks were thrown in the air, as were gloves, helmets, and other equipment. Tears sprang into the eyes of Negan and Dimitri Petrov. Even Brandon Thorpe, one of the most stoic men Chris had ever met, couldn't stop smiling. The Gators were upset, some even crying, for good reason. But they still lined up, they still shook hands, and they skated off in silence, giving the shitty ice to the Gulls to celebrate.

The commissioner, a man everyone hated because of a long-standing tradition, came out, made a speech, and presented Brandon Thorpe the Stanley Cup. Everyone booed during the speech—as was tradition—and the majority of the fans started to exit the stadium while others, even Gators fans, stayed to watch the festivities.

Brandon was given the Cup first. He was captain and he played a damn fine series; a damn fine playoffs. Chris watched with amusement as Brandon, now without his mask and his gloves, took the Cup and hoisted it over his head, skating up and down the ice before handing it over to Zachary Ryan.

From there, Brandon did something nobody expected. Once he handed the Cup off, he skated straight to the bench where Seraphina Hanson—owner and manager of the team—stood, clapping and cheering next to her older sister, Katella, and pulled her into a deep kiss. Chris couldn't stop himself from smiling. Everyone on the team knew these two were together, even if they thought they were hiding it. They were doing a shitty job of it; the way they looked at each other, the way they accidentally touched each other, it was obvious for someone like Chris—who had never considered himself as being in love before—to see.

Soon, the team was doing surprising displays of affection: Negan swept Katella up and skated with her around the ice as she pounded on his back; Kyle Underwood dropped to his knees so he could give the now-showing Emma a kiss on her stomach; Alec kissed his girl; Drew Stefano, Art Jackman, Dean Morgan, and Zachary Ryan pulled their women in passionate embraces.

The person who surprised Chris the most was Dimitri Petrov, who pulled the red-headed former Ice Princess into a kiss, with his kids right there. Chris knew Dimitri was going through his own divorce—and he was too good-looking to stay single for very long—but to see him with someone who was clearly younger than he was, was a bit of a shock.

"Good for you," Chris murmured to himself.

It took a moment before Chris got his turn. When Matt Peters handed him the Cup, his hands tingled. It was heavier than he expected it to be, but Chris didn't waver. He hoisted it over his head, just as everyone else had done, and skated the length of the ice. Before he passed it off to Solis, still on injury reserve after a cheap hit in an early-series game, he brought it to his lips and kissed it.

There was no one waiting for him, save for his sister, Isadora. He grinned when he saw her and embraced her. She hugged him back before pulling away and smacking his shoulder.

"God, you smell," she said. "Did Dad teach you nothing about taking care of your smelly equipment?"

Chris nodded, pulling Isadora closer to him by tossing one arm over her shoulder. "Damn straight," he said. "He taught me the value of superstition. I haven't washed these in years."

Isa pushed him off of her once more, causing him to toss his head back and laugh.

"Kidding," he insisted. "Come on, kidding. You know i'm not superstitious."

She smiled but made no move to get closer to him. Chris couldn't blame her.

As he watched everyone find their families, he glanced up at the ceiling. He wished his father had been here to see this, but his father had been gone for two years now. No matter. Once it was summer and he could fly home to Michigan, he would visit his father's grave with the Cup and tell him everything.

But not now. It was not a time to mourn. It was a time to celebrate. He could hear his father's voice even now berating him for turning an important moment sappy and then the light slap to the back of his head to ensure his point sank in. Chris chuckled at the thought, sinking in.

"Wish you had someone to make out with now that you're a champion?" Isa asked, crossing her arms over her chest to give the team a quizzical look.

"You don't have to be so judgmental, you know," Chris chided her. "And to answer your question, I am perfectly content being single. I plan to drink until I can't throw up anymore, buy a tiger, and maybe leave Solis up on the roof of a hotel."

"As long as you wear a fanny pack, you do you." She slapped his back supportively.

"Satchel," he corrected. "It's a satchel."

Before Isa could respond, the NHL Commissioner walked back to the podium.

"Congratulations go to the Newport Beach Seagulls," he said. "Now, I'll let Seraphina Hanson take the podium." He stepped back and looked to Seraphina, who was still wrapped up in Brandon's arms.

She felt her lips curl up and pulled away from Brandon to carefully make her way on the ice. Luckily, there was a narrow carpet which had been rolled out so she could walk on the ice in those heels without slipping and falling. When she reached the podium, she placed a hand on either side and smiled.

"Um, honestly, I hadn't expected to say anything so I'm not really prepared," she said. "Obviously, I want to say thank you to the Florida Gators, and the competitive games they played against us were entertaining, to say the least. This Cup, this belongs to the players and the coaches. But more than that, every single person of the organization deserves their share of the credit. From the security guards to the secretaries to Cherney and everyone else, this is yours. My grandfather—" she stopped abruptly, her voice catching as tears filled her eyes. She cleared her throat. "My grandfather would have been so proud of each and every one of you. Congratulations, Gulls. *We did it!*"

Brandon Thorpe was announced as Most Valuable Player, another award that was well-deserved. Unlike Seraphina, Brandon opted to not make a speech, which was fine. He didn't need to. His play spoke for itself.

Chris glanced up at the stands. Over half the stadium was empty, but the Gulls fans were at the glass, pounding, shouting, crying, and laughing.

*I wish you were here, Dad,* he thought to himself. *You would have enjoyed this almost as much as I do.*

After the festivities, the team lined up behind Thorpe and skated one more time around the rink, waving, smiling, and thanking their fans. Chris tried to memorize this moment, this feeling, not wanting to forget one second of it years from now when he was old and gray.

It was official. The Newport Beach Sea Gulls were Stanley Cup champions. Now, it was time to party.

\*\*\*

Want the next book in the Slapshot Series? Book 8 is available here! Grab it now!

## Stay up to date!

Book 8, the as of yet unnamed book in The Slapshot Series, will be released September 21, 2018.

Want updates on when my latest book comes out, exclusive giveaways, and free stuff? Sign up for my newsletter here!

# Did You Like Brutal Love & Stanley Cups?

As an author, the best thing a reader can do is leave an honest review. I love gathering feedback because it shows me you care and it helps me be a better writer. If you have the time, I'd greatly appreciate any feedback you can give me. Thank you!

## Acknowledgments

The Anaheim Ducks because they're my team no matter what - especially the team from 2011. My inaugural season. ;)

My family

My friends

Jammie for your AMAZING betas!

Susanna Lynn, for your beautiful cover. It's amazing and stunning and perfect!

Theresa Schultz, my amazing and hilarious editor.

Thank you to my readers who have fallen in love with this series, with hockey, and with the amazing players. I write for YOU!

Frank, Kylee & Madisyn, Josh & Jacob, for your continued love, support, and understanding

Manufactured by Amazon.ca
Acheson, AB

12206704R00098